Disc

The Cactus Growers' (Unless otherwise indic characters, businesses, in this book are either t author's imagination or used in a fictitious manner. The global pandemic, however, has been very real.

Mabel & Stanley Publishing

MABEL & STANLEY
PUBLISHING

For my family

Chapter 1

"I will not worry about things I cannot control; I will not worry about things I cannot control; I WILL NOT WORRY about things I cannot control."

My friend Paula had given me a set of affirmation cards recently, they were a going-away present and I am throwing myself on their mercy to convince myself that I am completely in control of my life. I need something to allay my growing sense of panic as I am sitting on the Irish Ferries W.B. Yeats from Holyhead to Dublin Port. A poetic name for this carrier of crowds, conveyors, and commodities. The car deck had been palpably thick with the whiff of diesel and car fumes but, climbing the passenger stairwell, had brought a more perfumed aroma of furniture polish along with a faint, alluring scent of coffee and what smelt like the frazzle of an all-day breakfast from the buffet. Finally, arriving at the main doors, I had felt a welcome glare of natural daylight, like a miner returning to the surface of a coal pit.

The main passenger deck is bright, the brass handrails of the main staircase reflecting in the illuminated screens of the slot machines, creating a myriad of shimmers on the recently polished glass aimed at enticing fatigued travellers to part with their money. Two or three lone characters had already mounted their high stools in front of the flickering and chiming no-armed bandits, utterly enticed, whilst tossing their carry-on bags aside and intent on conquering the big pay-out. Such diversions do not hold any allure for me.

I scan the information board at the foot of the grand stairway that climbs and divides in two for passengers to ascend to the balcony and pre-booked seating. Things have changed a lot since I last boarded a ferry to travel to Ireland. The muted colours of the seating, the plush carpets, the marbled effect on the walls and the panels of mink dark glass. This feels like a much bigger and more elaborate adventure than a three-hour spin across the Irish Sea. There is a cinema and a variety of cafes and eateries filled with fellow travellers. I let myself drift away for a few moments, imagining that I am heading off to a sun-drenched, island paradise on a cruise ship, but that inviting image is cut short abruptly when I have to gingerly step over the feet of several snoring lorry drivers who have "bedded down" on the sofas next to the coffee shop. "So much for white sandy beaches," I say to myself in a whisper, so that I do not wake these sleeping beauties. I consider establishing "base camp" on one of the few seats remaining, but remembering the long drive, and the remaining drive to come, decide that maybe this is the time to take in my surroundings and stretch my legs further than 90 degrees.

I walk out onto the external deck and look back towards the island of Anglesea and the port of Holyhead. The water is whisked up into white, foam trails emanating from the ferry, each one like a dissolving memory of where this huge ship had been on the water, then once again disappearing into the grey-blue of the sea. I hope that my new journey will be one where the turbulence of the past few months is made smooth again. Gulls are following the ferry, seemingly floating rather than flying. They look so effortless and elegant and free, what it must be to be able to glide and rise as they do. I remain rooted on my temporary ground.

I know that my decision to make this move may be considered as rash by some. Certifiably crazy by my friends Paula and Sue. *Note to self, "Let the girls know when I reach Dublin."*

Crazy or not, I need something new, and I need to stop feeling how I had felt since my aunt had died six months ago. She had always been a bundle of energy and fun, until cancer had taken a hold on her three years ago. My years of nursing did little to help, other than to keep her comfortable in her final weeks and with me as long as possible. The day I lost her still seems like yesterday. I can clearly remember the moment she left, one breath of life and then nothing. I am not a spiritual person but there is that moment when the life force leaves a body and I have reimagined that painful exit every day for the last six months. That is why I needed to do something different, be somewhere different. A way of reinventing myself and writing a new chapter in my life. My friends have their own stories to find and follow and, as I do not have any siblings or immediate family, I need to turn into this new stage. A sense of liberation and anticipation. This is a brave new world for my 45-year-old self. I read recently, 'It takes courage to grow up and become who you really are,'[1] and this is me trying to do just that, with a mix of courage and just a bit of recklessness thrown in for good measure.

I had spent time considering my options and settled upon this move to Ireland after finding old photos of my dad as a young man. He had grown up in north County Dublin when it was still a rural place covered by patchworks of fields. We had enjoyed family holidays there when I was young, and I have wonderful memories of a wholesomeness and community I now

1 E.E.Cummings

find it hard to see in my part of England. I know that I need to find a place to heal and to make sense of what life means to me.

Despite the brilliance of the early afternoon, the chill of the sea breeze nips at my face, and I can feel the salt in the air, like a faint mist of brine. I hear the churn of the engines of the ferry and look at the water below, the wake of the ferry appearing gelatinous and undulating. Everything else is quiet in my head. On opening the deck door, my ears are assailed with the clink of teacups, the munch of sandwiches and the chatter of my fellow passengers. I can hear in the background the faint hum of the ferry engines rumble on as I purchase my tea and continue to say to myself, “I will not worry about things I cannot control,” all the while feeling very worried indeed!

The three-hour crossing is concluding, and an announcement blasts out on the decks that we will be arriving shortly in the Port of Dublin and that passengers must get ready to return to their vehicles. A crowd start to gather at the stairwell doors leading below to the car deck. A servile flock waiting for the command to move downwards from the tannoy. I look around me at my fellow voyagers and indulge myself in some fleeting people watching. Lorry drivers with their rucksacks, couples with young children, who look as though they have brought the contents of a small toy shop with them on the trip to keep their little darlings entertained, older passengers with small wheelie cases, flasks protruding from their hand luggage. All shapes and sizes and dispositions, all about to venture off the ferry for work, holiday or in my case, a new life adventure.

The doors are opened by the crew and this diverse and rag-tag group of passengers make their way down the stairs. The lorry drivers lope down the flights quickly, keen to be in their cabs and on their way - after all time is money and they could be heading anywhere across the island of Ireland - whatever their destination, it needs to be reached quickly and cost efficiently; the tachometer never lies.

The less experienced travellers are a little more circumspect about making their way down the steps. The ferry is still moving and the less steady of the descending mass are hanging on the handrails with a fierce determination that does not reconcile well with the growing crowd behind them. I am not really in a desperate rush to move on, final tiny doubts are in my mind and this ferry could be the last time I am in a "limbo" state for some time. When I drive off the ferry, that will be it, I will have arrived, and all my thinking and rational planning will have to kick in.

Back to my dark grey VW Golf sitting on the car deck of this poet, dramatist, writer and seagoing vessel. It is filled with essentials; bags, boxes, bulging with trappings of a life gone and a life still to live. The cabin of the car packed like a sardine can with contents wedged so tightly that there is barely room to breathe, let alone for me to get into the driver's seat. The contents represent what I consider to be critical to my new existence in my new country. I suppose it does not really amount to very much; bags and boxes filled with bits and pieces I think I will need. I still have my furniture in storage, but that will be for another time, as my rented apartment comes furnished and is only a one bedroom. From the photos, I do not anticipate much room to swing a cat let alone the contents of a three-bed semi; so bags and boxes only for now. The apartment is billed as being in a "leafy area" of Dublin near to the Phoenix Park and the name resonates with me as a place to redefine myself like a mythical phoenix, but probably more like an oven-ready chicken at the moment.

"First things first," I say to my reflection in the rear-view mirror. "Time to get off this ship and to sort my life out, no point in worrying about anything until it is a reality." I feel scared, I feel brave but most of all, I feel as though this is the most daunting thing I have ever taken upon myself. I start the engine and can hear all the other cars, lorries, vans and motorhomes doing the same thing. An image of the old cartoon the "Whacky Races" comes into my head, and I smile to myself. Time to go.

The huge doors of the car deck slowly open, a gaping maw leading onto the dock road. Firstly, just a crack of light, then further opening to reveal a bright, late afternoon. The wispy cirrus clouds are stretching across the sky and gulls flying over the port. There the scenic impression ends. The Port of Dublin welcomes ferries and vast numbers of transport tankers and vessels. The place is stacked with containers in reds, blues and yellows – like a huge Lego construction set that is created and broken down by the gantry cranes that move the containers from ship to shore and then onto the drayage trucks and then back again. The cranes seem to reveal a glimpse into an industrial mechanised world, their movement leaving the air with a hum of greeting to the newly arrived ferries, tankers and sea barges. A metal clad circle of life, bringing food and goods from all over the world. Just beyond this industrial landscape and the expanse of concrete, I can still see the River Liffey and sailing boats moored. It will be good to be on dry land and, after the official checks of Port security, I will be on my way. After all my recent misgivings, I feel optimistic and am reminded of the affirmation cards that Paula gave me.

"There are no blocks I cannot overcome," I say aloud. "That's right watch out blocks because you are dust!" I say, before crunching the gears on my beloved Golf, narrowly missing a bollard, and getting a warning shout from one of the Port stewards.

I take my opportunity to pull into the side of the road before I exit the enclave of the port authority. I have had a fascination with ports since I visited Liverpool with my father when I was a child. They seem to be places layered with purpose and this one is my springboard into a new life. I enter the address of my letting agent Mr O'Connor at the Parkside Properties Management Company into the maps app on my phone, set it into its cradle and set off on the journey to collect my keys.

As I exit the port and turn right towards the quays, I face new buildings clad in steel and glass that seem at odds with the brickwork of the Three Arena behind them, once the depot for trams, and now the venue for bands. I am slightly taken aback that the warm and fuzzy memories I have of trips to Dublin are just pure nostalgia, maybe this whole venture is simply a crazy leap into the unknown. I shake my head, trying to put any negative thoughts to one side for now.

"No Blocks!"

I head alongside the River Liffey as it glints and shimmers in the late afternoon. The further I progress along the quays I see other new buildings; it is staggering that so much has been built so quickly. The glossy facades of the new Dublin displaying the corporate logos of international businesses that have taken residence here. These names are instantly recognisable and, for a moment, I could be in any city in Europe. Oh, how Dublin has changed. As I continue, I begin to see the older buildings, the places I remember from my childhood ventures. I think I prefer the older, rougher brickwork where the bricks seem barely held together by the ageing mortar. I guess that I am just an old-fashioned girl at heart. I must turn to cross the Liffey at the Talbot Memorial Bridge and venture to the south of the river. Old and new are juxtaposed here as well, with random groups of people some meandering along and some waiting at the rank of bus stops as the traffic edges towards O'Connell Bridge.

Drivers seem a bit more calm here than I have been used to in England. I am sure that this is a busy time, but I feel quite relaxed and even grasp an opportunity to admire the Ha'Penny Bridge in all its 19th Century splendour, home to the homeless, trying to get the price of a room in a hostel for the night. The River Liffey glimmers and reflects distorted images of the buildings flanking its span.

The next minutes are spent creeping along in Thursday afternoon traffic, passing convenience stores and burger joints and the infamous Temple Bar area. This is the picture postcard Dublin, with narrow lanes promising late night pints, live music, frolics and of course, “the craic,” that the Irish capital is so well known for. I am sure that it would not take long to get to know the area and to feel at home. Despite having residual nerves, I feel that I can most definitely “do this.”

Past the magnificent domed façade of the Four Courts, past the huge Viking Ship that rests just to the side of the Dublin City Council offices, the old and new buildings managing to appear more in accord than the more recent developments adjacent to the port. Closer and closer to my destination according to the navigator on my phone. Now the smell, that malty smell of James’ Gate Brewery. The legendary, black-gated home of the famous drink from Ireland. This means that I am close to my destination, and I turn right at Heuston Station to head towards the Phoenix Park. At the traffic lights, my car is the only vehicle turning. I check my map again; just a little further and I will be there. And there it is! The Parkside Property Management Company, well there it was! Nowhere to park and sucked into traffic, where the hell did it all come from?

“Recalculating,” says the maps app, “Recalculating.”

“Just bloody be quick about it!” I respond, not really wanting to keep following a road I do not know and because I realise that the letting agent will soon be shutting up shop for the evening and then I will be left bedding down in my very cramped car.

“Take the next left,” this time with a little authority from the Google Map co-pilot.

Indicator on, left is taken and I find myself in what is possibly the narrowest road I have ever driven down. What is even more stupefying is that it is a two-way road! I have never really had occasion to use the expression *goad your loins,* but this appears to be one of those times and that’s exactly what I do! I do not care if anything is coming the other way, or the abuse I will inevitably get, but I position myself in the middle of the double-parked cars and go for it. The road bears round to the left and I am thinking that this is the traffic planning that time forgot when I discover that I have driven full circle and am back facing the sign of the letting agent! Five minutes before the shutters go down and still to find a parking space.

"You've got this," I say again to myself. And then, divine intervention as a space opposite me magically becomes vacant.

My arrival at the office of the letting agent can only be described as a white knuckle "just in time" event. Opening the door of my Golf, I feel as though I am coming up for air after being in a sealed chamber. I barely manage to beat the shutters descending between me and the keys to my new flat ... "Is it a flat or an apartment?" I muse to myself as I wait for Mr O'Connor the letting agent to get the final paperwork and most importantly the keys to my new "kingdom." He is not best pleased with my timekeeping and standing in the way of whatever delights this evening holds for him. The front window has lots of rental properties on display, and I see my future home has a sticker "RENTED" on it, rented to me!

"You are lucky you got me Ms Moore," he says as he rifles through the letting documentation, "I am very strict about punctuality... I realise that may not be the way of things now, but punctuality is the virtue of men of business, and the graceful courtesy of princes..."

I fear that this is not the first time he has recited this mantra and feel just a little put into the naughty corner. I feel an uncomfortable blush creeping up from my collar towards my face, I've never been good with being reprimanded even if it was done in such a "*quote-phile*" way.

"There we are that is everything," he says, "If you could sign here and here and oh yes, here for the disclaimer for property damage, yes that's the one."

I take the pen and sign where he indicates and then get that tingle of excitement again when I get the key in my hand. This is all very real now. So, Mr O'Connor of the Parkside Property Management Company, has just created another huge milestone in a day that has already looked like Stonehenge. The final review for bank transfer details and that is it. In this small office next to the Phoenix Park, I am taking a step forward.

Mr O'Connor shakes my hand, "I hope you will be happy here Ms Moore, you know the Phoenix Park is one of the largest enclosed parks in Europe and it is all on your doorstep – a chance for new beginnings as I always say to my clients."

I am a little taken aback. Mr O'Connor's initial gruffness, on account of my tardiness, had perhaps led me to misjudge him somewhat. Perhaps his gruff exterior masks a perceptive gift; if anyone needs a new beginning then it is most definitely me.

Mr O'Connor gives me the directions to the property - Grove House, flat number 4 - and both his mobile number and the number of the building maintenance company. I say my goodbyes to Mr O'Connor and, as I leave the office, I see there is a corner shop a few doors away. Just a quick trip in to get milk, bread, eggs, cereal, tea and maybe a celebratory bar of chocolate. As I walk up to the front door, it opens smoothly with a swoosh and the glare of the lights illuminate a huge range of food and household goods. This place hints at having everything I need and maybe a lot I do not. I am delighted it is so close for those last-minute things I always seemed to be forgetting to buy in recent months. I used to be incredibly organised, but loss had taken its toll in so many ways, including losing the ability to put together a shopping list. I take a basket and gather up my first night haul, including a few bits to add to the eggs to make an omelette. I hear raised voices over near the till.

"Ah here Jim this is the last time, you really cannot come in here dressed like that," says the dark-haired young woman behind the till; her carefully applied makeup and diamanté ear cuffs lending the whole ensemble a level of glitz at odds with her red, uniform t-shirt.

I look over to Jim. He is standing with a pair of pyjamas at half mast, a pair of green "Crocs" and the grubbiest, tie-dyed t- shirt I think I have ever seen. He mutters something I cannot make out; this “reality tv” version of the local mini market shop is unfolding before my eyes.

Once again, the young woman behind the counter with the ear cuffs, issues her warning, “Jim, do I have to get security to haul up those bleedin’ kecks or do you think you’ll find yer way to covering that fat rear end of yours?”

This seems to have the desired effect and Jim grabs the waistband of the gravity ridden “Kecks” and pulls them up with a dramatic flourish. His face breaks into a smile as he politely asks for a packet of cigarettes and a can of Red Bull. As he lifts his purchases from the counter the princess asks, “So where are you heading now Jim?”

He replies, “Nowhere,” before he exits the swooshing doors.

“Yeh, thought so,” she responds.

I am the only customer in the shop and, as I take my basket to the counter, I see that her name is Keira. I smile to myself that this name would be perfect for a social media blogger and put my items down before her.

“How’s it going?” Keira enquires, as she starts to scan the items with a beep as each one is illuminated with the bright red light of the till scanner.

“Good thanks,” I reply.

"Are you English? I've an aunt living in Luton, you from anywhere nearby there? I've been there a couple of times for weddings but only briefly, would love to head over again my aunt is great craic." All this information delivered while she deftly piles up my "messages" as she calls them. I think this is the most conversation I have ever had at a shop till, and it takes me by surprise.

I reply with a "Yes, not really, great to catch up with family."

I pay for my shopping and Keira asks what my plans are. "I am just moving in," there it is a declaration of my intent. A public commitment to this change and it is beginning to feel good. I thank her and turn towards the swooshing doors.

"Thanks a million, see you soon," she calls.

Chapter 2

I have my provisions, I have my keys, I have no idea exactly where my new home is but in the words of the song, "Two out of three ain't bad." I debate whether to key the address into my phone or to try and find out where I need to go the old-fashioned way; by asking a real person. I decide to take the brave option and look around to see if I can find a likely candidate to give directions. My eyes alight on a man who looks to be in his thirties. He has a blue rucksack on his back and is pushing a rented bike along. I decide to go for it.

"Excuse me?" I ask.

No reply. "Excuse me, I wonder if you might be able to help me?" I try again.

He puts his hand to his ear and removes an ear bud, I had not noticed because he is wearing a hat.

"Oh, I am sorry," he says, "did you want something? I could not hear you with the music." He smiles at me.

"I wonder if you might know where this place is," I ask, "I wanted to check before I try to move my car again, parking is a bit of a nightmare around here!"

"You are not wrong," he grins. "That's why I hire a two-wheeler whenever I need one," he pats the handlebars of his trusty rented steed. "Yes, the place you are looking for is about 6 houses down on the left side of the road, I think that it has a dark green door you will find it easily; nice to meet you." With that he continues on his way, and I start to walk in the direction he pointed.

The properties on this road must have been quite magnificent in their heyday. Each one, three stories over basement with stairs leading up to the front door. They look slightly less glamorous now and, of the houses I pass, three are boarded up with hoardings and one is decidedly seedy with brown, tattered net curtains. There is a buddleia growing out of part of the roof and it has an air of not having been loved for many years. Then yes, this is mine. It is indisputably past its best but, at least the paintwork looks fresh, the gravel inside the fence looks tidy and the front door is indeed green with a brass handle. I take a closer look. The bricks are russet and solid, ruddy, red; bringing a warm appearance to the exterior of the building. Some of the mortar is a little pockmarked but the overall impression is very pleasing.

The sash windows are not original, which jars slightly with the traditional frontage, lending lidded eyes towards me, gazing out onto the road below, implacable. The thing I notice most is the stone staircase rising to the shared front door. It has obviously been there for generations and as I gaze at the steps, I ponder for a moment about the people who have visited through the years and the stories those stairs have been a bit part player in. A stone banister runs up along the stairs with a carved finial at the base. The stone is pitted, and in places there is a faint algae growth, introducing a mottled orange and green to the greyness. I wonder how many hands have touched the finials; ah the power of inanimate objects to encourage you to take a trip into imagination.

"All that's missing is a bit of greenery," I say aloud to myself.

My eyes scale the front of Grove House, taking in the full facade of my new home. My vision reaches the top floor and I see not one, not two, not even three cacti, but all the windows are crammed with every imaginable size and shape of prickly plant in every window. I try to count them but realise that they are double-lined along the windowsills making it impossible to really see how many of the spiny succulents are living side by side. Someone is obviously dedicated to whatever a cacti collector is known as (I make a mental note to find that nugget of information out). The other windows do not render as much interest for me, and my eyes return to the cacti congregation. I wonder who the cactus collector is and what their fascination for these savagely prickly house plants could be. I feel something wet dripping on my right foot and look down to see the milk carton I purchased is weeping steadily and it is time for me to get sorted out and let myself in to my own corner of Grove House.

I climb the stairs to the dark green front door adorned with the brass handle in the middle. The metal has a patina of years of use. There is an ornate fanlight above the door with ironwork fleur-de-lis over the glass. Each step has a curved capstone. The first step is slightly uneven being worn in the middle with a sheen of the years of people ascending. The next two steps are also worn to a shine, like someone has polished them with a buffing machine. Each one of the steps about a metre wide makes me feel as though I am truly making a grand entry through this grand entrance. Another three steps and I am at the porch and the front door – I feel like I might be a Jane Austen heroine - albeit I am missing the long dress, hat, youth and being reliant on a wealthy benefactor; if only! To the left of the door there is a set of buttons with flat numbers written, no names though.

I take the set of keys out of my pocket and look to see which one fits the front door. The medium sized one of the three fits and, as I turn it, the catch clicks and I push the door open. The door is heavy and solid and opens into the red and black tiled hallway that runs to the back of the building. The main indicators that the place has been converted into flats is the green and white emergency exit sign suspended from the ceiling and on the wall there are signs explaining fire regulations and meeting points, along with handwritten signs advertising a community garden tidy up group and a dog walking service. I can hear faint murmurs from televisions and radios - maybe conversations - but it is too difficult to distinguish as they are indistinct and muffled.

I see that flats number one and two are on the ground floor, so head up to the first floor to find my new abode. The stairs are carpeted with a dark carpet that I suspect would be under the "for stairs and areas of heavy tread" section in a carpet showroom. I always think that sounds very practical but imagine a herd of domestic elephants trampling on what my dad always referred to as "the pile." There is a decorative fleck in the carpet, but it retains that quintessential "hard wearing" feel to it. The walls are painted white, and the bannisters are gloss-varnished wood and it looks very promising as I reach the landing outside my flat. Again, a quick check to see which key is the right one and then I am in!

Chapter 3

I walk through the front door of Flat Number 4.

"Moore, Flat 4," I smile to myself. "Moore inside the door of Flat 4."

The flat has pristine white emulsion walls. I walk straight into the living room from the landing and the space is bathed in late afternoon sunshine. The furniture comprises a small pale green sofa, white coffee table, a bookshelf with a lamp, a small square table and two chairs. Everything is light, bright, and fresh looking. The kitchen is a small, galley-style set up with the emphasis on minimal and clean lines, the fridge freezer is spotlessly clean and although the space is small, everything is well-appointed. This all suits me perfectly and I see there is ample storage space which is welcome when I think of my packed Golf down the road. On the coffee table there is another "In case of fire" information sheet for the residents plus an especially important residents parking disc for the spaces to the rear of Grove House.

I leave my food shopping (including the dripping milk on a saucer) in the fridge and head out with the keys and my parking disc in hand to collect my car. I am not looking forward to unpacking and bringing everything upstairs, but it is an unavoidable task so I resolve to get everything sorted as quickly and efficiently as I can.

As I leave the flat, I see the door opposite open just a faint crack. I feel eyes taking me in and I look directly back.

"Hello," I say, "I'm your new neighbour, just moving in now."

No reply.

"My name is Angie, Angie Moore," I continue. "This is a lovely old house."

The door opens fractionally more, and I see the face of a woman, it looks like she is in her early thirties, but it is hard to tell because her dark hair is hanging over her face and her whole-body language whispers shyness. She looks up and as her hair parts slightly, I notice that she has the most startling green eyes. She is wearing a pale pink t shirt and what I think are black leggings, but it is difficult to see as the door is still not much further ajar.

“Hello,” she says with some effort. “Nice to meet you, there has not been anyone in number four for a while. I’m Sinead.”

“Good to meet you Sinead,” I reply, “I am just heading down to move my car and to move my....” She is gone. I am a bit taken aback at the abrupt close to our first conversation, but everyone is different, and I have a feeling that there may be more to Sinead’s story, but that it is one that may reveal itself slowly.

Back down the stairs and out the door to retrieve my trusty Golf. The traffic is quieter now and I have no problem negotiating the turn to get to the parking area at the back of Grove House. There are two cars already parked there, a slightly knocked around metallic blue Renault Clio with a 10 D numberplate, and a dark red CW Toyota Yaris. The area is gravelled and has weeds poking through the stones. Tall trees form a dappled cover of shadows moving in the slight breeze as the last trailing fingers of sunshine reach through to try to touch the ground. The area under the trees is a wilderness; overgrown with scrub and nettles, a stark contrast with the tidy gravelled space.

The unpacking is less challenging than I expect. I had implemented all my near Olympic standard Tetris skills in loading the car with not one scrap of space wasted and much to my amazement, everything seems to work in the reverse. The big challenge is to get the bags and boxes up the stairs again. This time there is no sense of a Jane Austen heroine, more a sense of a slave in Tolkien's pits of Mordor!

If I had seen any of my neighbours I may have asked for a bit of help, but neither Sinead nor the other residents make any appearance so there are eleven return journeys to move my possessions up the stairs. I am exhausted! What a day! The last trip up the stairs is so very welcome and I make a cup of tea and reflect how grateful I am that I have given myself a couple of days before I start work at "The Beeches" nursing home down the road.

My thoughts go to food. My stomach is rumbling loudly, and I make a quick omelette seasoned with salt and pepper. I am so hungry that it barely touches the sides of my mouth as I eat.

I suddenly remember that I had promised to let Paula and the girls know when I had arrived. I pick up my mobile and make the calls. Paula first.

Ring Tone.

"Hi Paula? It's Angie. I have arrived!"

She sounds relieved, "Angie I am so pleased to hear from you I've been worried that something bad had happened to you."

Paula is a bit of a worrier. I think that is why she became interested in her colourful and positive affirmation cards.

She is an advocate of declaring to the world that everything is going to be fine, although I know that she secretly has unsaid doubts all the time.

"Yes, everything is grand. Just finished getting all my stuff in from the car and have had something to eat. The flat is nice, small but nice, and the house it is in, well let me just say that it would not look out of place in a period drama."

"Excuse me, did you just say "grand" Angie?" Paula asks through a giggle.

"Did I? I guess I did."

"You're acclimatising quickly! I will not know you to talk to after a week!" Paula laughs again.

I am going to miss our coffees and face to face chats, but I am hoping that she may be able to come over for a visit soon and by that stage I will have hopefully kissed the Blarney Stone!

We say our goodbyes and promise to catch up soon so that I can tell her all about my new job. The flat seems to fill with silence once we have finished our call. Like a blanket of peacefulness being gently pulled up and tucked into the corners of the room. I decide to text the other girls, I know that Paula will give them a reassuring update as well, and I realise that I am hitting a wall of fatigue after my day of travelling.

It is dusk outside, and I open the window to listen to the sounds of this new city. There is a low rumbling noise, not traffic but something a little more in the distance and not really a mechanical tone. It is not a sound I recognise and as quickly as it starts it stops again. I strain to hear if the noise reoccurs but there is little more than the sound of the occasional car and the birds starting to roost in the trees along the road. I feel tired but happy, this has been the first day of new things for me and so far, so good. I will have the opportunity to explore tomorrow... adventure beckons!

Chapter 4

I am disorientated when I wake. The previous day's travel and such huge changes in my situation has been nothing less than shattering both physically and emotionally. I have lived my whole life in a house of one sort or another, but this is the first time I have ventured into the world of flats, and it is a new experience to hear the variety of sounds vaguely suggesting the kettles, radios and televisions from the morning routines of the other residents. It is 7.45 am and from what I am hearing, it sounds as though most of the people living here in Grove House have places to go, people to see and livings to earn. That will be me tomorrow. Today comes first though and I will decide on my plan after I have made a cup of tea.

There is a noise above me. Music is playing, not loudly, but there is an exotic percussion accent to it. I hear steps and strain to listen; dancing! At 7.45 am! I am counting the steps in my head one, two, three, four. I can hear the distinctive rhythm of the maracas and suddenly in my mind's eye I am magically transported to Cuba, whilst having my breakfast on the North Circular Road. Then I realise the dancer is also the owner of the cacti; now this is becoming even more intriguing and I know I will definitely have to discover who my mysterious upstairs neighbour is. I feel as though I should be eating something far more cosmopolitan, or at least be sitting next to one of those candy-coloured Cadillacs in Havana, but it's just me and the strawberry jam on toast I am having with my mug of tea.

The music continues for a little while and the syncopated steps continue. It is not loud or annoying, just interesting to hear the pattern of another's morning taking shape and clearly involving dancing into the day. I have never been much of a dancer but there is something in the cadenced paces overhead that makes me feel that I should maybe give it a go. Something else to investigate and not yet 8.30 am in the day!

I finish my tea and all that remains on my plate are the crumbs of the toast. I wash up and make ready to head out and get a sense of my surroundings. The day looks mild and bright, and I shower, blow dry my hair and get dressed putting on the first things in the top of the suitcase. I turn to look at my reflection in the oblong mirror, turning this way and that. I decide I am not too bad for my age, maybe a few pounds that in a perfect world I could do without, but overall, not bad. I had been to the hairdresser before making my trip and my hair had been styled in a pixie cut with ash blond and caramel highlights. This is the shortest my hair has been in years, but I thought it would be practical for work and it is very flattering. T- shirt, jeans and a light jacket with just a faint application of makeup and I am ready!

I take the parking permit off the coffee table and leave number 4. No sign of life on the landing and no sign of my dancing neighbour from up the stairs. I decide I will walk, it's so much easier to take things in on foot and I do not want to waste the time negotiating traffic right now.

I head down towards the front door where I meet a man who looks to be about my own age. He has sandy blond hair that is cut in a short back and sides. His face bears the tan of a person who has had the opportunity to spend time in the summer sunshine and he has twinkly blue eyes. He is slim and stands about a foot taller than me. He is wearing faded blue jeans and a pressed checked green shirt. I see he is carrying a bag for life in one hand and a tiny Yorkshire terrier in the other. The little dog eyes me suspiciously and utters a very small, but threatening, growl. This is a strange picture indeed and I am surprised to see a dog being allowed to live in Grove House, but then I have not really studied the rules and regulations as I do not own a dog. I notice that the Yorkie is wearing a tiny, high visibility jacket, which seems a bit excessive given that it is early morning. I decide to engage this dog bearer. "Good morning," I say with a smile, "I am Angie Moore, I've just moved into Number 4 upstairs."

The man gives me a hasty glance whilst trying to retain his hold on the pocket-size pooch in day glow yellow.

"Hello," he replies, "I'm Mick, from Number 1. Oh, and this feisty fellow is Leopold Bloom, Leo for short," he rearranges the errant Leo once more. "Well Angie what is it that you do? I hear from your accent that you are from England, what brings you to Dublin?"

I know that I am going to have to acclimatise myself to this question. Although Dublin and Ireland are much more cosmopolitan than they were when I visited as a child, I know that there is an inherent curiosity here and people love to hear your story. I decide to give a very potted version, there is no need to furnish the ups and downs of the past few years.

"I have just moved over to start work down the road at The Beeches," I reply, "I am a nurse by training and have specialised in geriatric care for the past few years. I am not a stranger to Dublin though, my dad was Irish, and I spent many happy summers here as a child."

He looks at me with renewed interest. I think that my Irish credentials have piqued his curiosity. I do not get the same approachable feeling from Leo who is still looking as though he would be quite happy to snap if I moved any closer.

"The Beeches, the care home just down the road?" Mick asks. "My mam is in there; she is the reason why I have this little fella. Leo is her dog, but they are not allowed in The Beeches, and he needed a home so here we are. Between you and me he is not really supposed to be here either, that is why he is wearing the High Vis, if anyone asks, I tell them he is an assistance dog!"

I take a closer look at Leo, the rather bad-tempered Yorkie, and then at Mick who is trying to keep a straight face. When our eyes lock that is it, no possibility of concealing or containing the laughter. Leo does not look impressed, making it evident that he is in fact the least likely assistance dog candidate anyone would ever be likely to meet. Mick gives a wry grin, he looks kind, and clearly tolerates this tiny four-legged tyrant for the sake of his mum; I like him.

Another resident descends the staircase, could this be my salsa dancing, cacti growing enigma from the flat above mine? An older lady dressed in neon pink lycra, with her silver hair pulled into a tight chignon, approaches.

"Good morning, Ursula," Mick greets her with a nod. "You will certainly stop traffic today for sure in that outfit," he jokes.

"There is no point being here if you don't enjoy it," she replies, "I am revelling in my age, a lot of my friends did not get the opportunity, besides I was always told that pink is my colour."

"Good on you!" says Mick, as Ursula executes a rather lovely shimmy. "Oh Ursula, before I forget, this is Angie, she has just moved into Number 4, that's the one below you, isn't it?"

"Yes, it certainly is," Ursula replies, and she turns to face me. "I hope I did not disturb you this morning," she says, "I do an hour of salsa every other day, it keeps my heart happy, and my legs limber and at my age, you need every little bit of those things you can get!"

"Not at all!" I reply. I do not want to admit I had been listening to the muffled sound of the music and rather enjoyed it. I did not know how such an admission would be received; and after all it is only day one. Ursula gave a big wave and said that she was heading to her Tai Chi session in the park.

Mick could see the bemusement on my face.

"She is just a live wire," he said, "lives life to the full and seems to have a much busier calendar than anyone else in this place, could teach me a thing or two about being in the moment." I think that he may see something in my face, a fleeting memory of my own loss and decides to say nothing more.

"Look I need to make a move Angie, his lordship here is not very tolerant of hanging around and I think I have probably already outstayed the acceptable dawdling time. Welcome to Grove House, I hope that you will be happy here and I am sure that we will bump into each other either here, or at The Beeches when I visit my mam." With that, he rearranged Leo and headed out of the front door.

I had not had the opportunity to ask Mick about the cacti, but there would always be another day. So that's three of the other residents I have now met in some shape of form, four if you count the Leopold Bloom.

I head out of the door myself and again down the steps that I had rushed up and down the previous evening. I decide to turn right and walk down towards the large, stone gateposts of the Phoenix Park. When I walk through them there is a steep downward slope to my left and the road bends towards the right. Everything is green and lush. Despite being so close to the city centre, the air feels cleaner inside the gate. How could that be possible? Maybe it is just the open space and the expanse of grass. I continue to walk along the right-hand path which opens onto what seems to be the main avenue through the park. To my left, the road goes downhill to the main Park Gate and there is a huge memorial over the road. I remember seeing it as a child but cannot remember what it is called. Google is deployed.

"The Wellington Monument, more correctly known as the Wellington Testimonial. A monumental granite obelisk located in a large grass area in Phoenix Park, one of Europe's largest designed urban spaces. Designed by Sir Robert Smirke to commemorate Arthur Wellesley, the Duke of Wellington, who is reputed to have been born in Dublin, and his military victories."[2]

After a further scan through the Google results, I see that the monument is 62 metres tall and is the tallest obelisk in Europe. It looms before me, a granite spire stretching above the surrounding tree canopy. To my right I notice a flash of neon pink in the middle of a group of people seeming to move in slow motion. Their movements have a flow to them, precise and focussed like a reel of time- lapse film. There is Ursula completely immersed in motion in the middle of the Tai Chi group.

2 Source www.buildingsofireland.ie

The other participants are dressed more modestly, and she stands out like an exotic bird of paradise in their midst. She is resplendent in her distinctive pink outfit. I can tell that my aunt would have enjoyed Ursula's joie de vivre. This is a lady I want to get to know better. The methodical flowing movement of the Tai Chi continues, and I carry on walking along the main road bisecting the park. I am surprised that I do not feel lonely. This is the first time in a long time that I do not feel as though I am carrying a cloud with me, a cloud of loss and helplessness that has hung over me for such a long time. I have felt numb to so much in life in recent times and the encounters of the day so far, have made me feel as though I have a chance at reconnecting with the fun in life.

I walk a few more metres, and the front entrance to the zoo comes into view. Oh, I remember the zoo from my childhood visits. It was a big day out with a picnic punctuated with occasional showers of rain. I believe the place has had a huge makeover in the past few years, a modern facelift that was very much needed. Dublin Zoo is one of the oldest in the world and certainly has been a place of incredibly happy memories for me. I decide that this will be a place I will visit when I am a bit more settled. That is when I hear it. The noise that I heard last night. A grumbling and rumbling roar. The big cats! That is exactly what I heard when the city quietened, and the traffic diminished to a mere trickle. That is when the lion reminds us in feline tones why he is king of the jungle. Despite the words of the song the lion did not sleep *last* night!

In the distance I see a statue. It is a column and at the top there is a bird reaching towards the sky. The Phoenix. I think this is truly the right place for me to put down new roots and make a new beginning. Mythical birds, great cats and intriguing people for neighbours, what more could I want? I continue to walk down towards the statue. The joggers are jogging, and they come in various shapes and sizes and are travelling at many different speeds. The beginners trying to shed some pounds on a Couch To 5k programme; their faces set with grim determination that is being coloured by the tinge of effort and the sheen of perspiration as they make their way through the park. The more experienced runners looking so smooth in their movements with the sinews visible in their calves, as they pound the path barely breaking sweat. It is possible to tell who has progressed further in their running endeavours by their clothing. T shirts emblazoned with words and logos such as Dublin City Marathon, various athletics clubs, 10k Park Runs and then the iron man runners and triathlon runners; their clothing like a declaration both of achievement and intent. All running at different paces and different distances but moving forward. It makes me think about my aunt who always said movement is life. I guess any movement counts if it is one foot in front of another and hopefully in the right direction. A group of ladies approach moving at a pace, but not runners this time. I estimate these ladies are a little older than myself. They look smart but have not capitulated to the wearing of clinging running gear, opting instead for whatever the correct word for "sportswear" is without the lycra content. As they approach the volume increases. They are all talking simultaneously and incessantly. I am not sure if they are listening to each other but there is clearly a joy in the release of the day's niggles or achievements. They are all smiles and there is an aura of camaraderie that is palpable as they move towards and past me. There is also a fluidity to the group, with paces adjusting and the changing of walking companions as though to spread the opportunity for conversation and connection. No one remains on the periphery. These walking ladies look much happier than some of their faster counterparts, sharing the need to get out and be part of the world whilst taking their daily constitutional. I try to listen to snippets as they pass me, but it is all one mist of chatter and sound and one I am unable to fully tune into in the moments of closeness.

Time is moving on and I decide it is an opportune moment to turn and retrace my paces back to Grove House. I have seen a coffee place near the entrance to the park and think that this will be a great chance to have a coffee and watch the world go by for a bit longer. I also need to get my supermarket shopping done, my brief visit to the shop yesterday evening will not tide me over for long and there are definitely some essentials that I need in advance of starting work. I see the coffee place "Park Perks," there are a number of tables outside and a couple of them are free.

Park Perks is painted a lovely shade of pale teal, with creamy accents around the windows and door frame. There is bunting in candy colours looped under the eaves. It presents a lovely, gentle picture against the green grass and the huge surrounding trees. The menu in the window declares it is open for all styles of coffee and teas, hot chocolates, smoothies, soft drinks. There is a deal advertised for a coffee and a treat for €4.50. Always one for a bargain I decide that is the option for me. The bright exterior paintwork is echoed inside with soft creamy colours. The coffee machine is pale blue and stainless steel and the marble counter glints from attentive cleaning. I take the place in. It is like a film set coffee shop waiting for a cute meet to happen, the two leads bumping into each other as fortunate coincidence.

To the side of the till there is a display cabinet with scones, muffins, lemon slices, macaroons and chocolate brownies lit up in a way to tempt customers to say, “Oh and I will have one of them too please!”

I am lost in a bit of a reverie when the voice behind the counter says, “Angie?”

I start at my name. I know that Dublin is very connected, but surely to goodness I am not already known here by name? A head pops over the coffee machine and it is Mick. He is wearing an apron, bearing the coffee shop name against a dark blue background.

“I see you are doing a bit of local exploring,” he says.

“Yes, it is a beautiful walk through the centre of the park. It is very busy, I lost count of all the runners I saw. Oh, I also saw Ursula’s Tai Chi group going through their moves,” I reply and ask, “Where’s Leo?”

“Doggy Day Care, or as I like to think of it a high security twilight home for snappy little dogs,” Mick sighs. “I’d love to be able to bring him in here, but you have seen what he is like, he would terrorise all the customers and I would probably be sued for ankle biting or some such thing. I look after him for mam’s sake and truth be told I am very fond of the little fella, but he does not make it easy to love him!”

I nod, even my very brief encounter with Leo had left me with a good sense of his total lack of interpersonal skills. I suppose he had been with Mick's mum and probably spoilt rotten for most of his life and now he is dressed like an 80's fitness guru in neon yellow and must go to doggy day-care. He clearly does not understand why he has been abandoned by the woman who has indulged him for all these years. Probably not the future he had imagined for himself and not one he seems ready to accept without complaint.

It could be seen as a sad state of affairs really and, if I was in my old mindset, I would be dwelling on it, but in the here and now I know that I want a coffee and one of those lovely looking scones with jam and cream and I just will not take on anything that will flatten my mood of optimism today. As my wise friend Paula has been known to say... "Not my circus, not my monkeys!"

I decide on a skinny latte (to compensate for the cream with the scone, who am I kidding!) and wait while Mick expertly renders a beautiful coffee in a proper cup. He plates up the fabulously risen scone, pops pots of cream and jam on the plate and hands it to me with a flourish.

I decide to sit outside and do some people watching, nice to have the time to take things in and to have the unhurried space for a change.

I choose a table that is partially shaded by a large oak tree. I love the shape of oak leaves. Thousands of ruffles of green on such majestic trees. I recall that the oak represents strength and protection and indeed, it looks as though its bows are reaching over to shelter café's patrons from the elements. I place my latte and scone on the table and take a quick look around me. Immediately next to me there is a young mother with her baby in a buggy; I see she also has a slightly older child who is running around chasing after pigeons, landing next to the tables to scrounge crumbs from the ground. The baby is sleeping, and the mum is sipping at her tea.

"Look Mammy, look!!!!" the little boy scampers up to his mum with a look of pure joy on his face. "Did you see Mammy? I chases off the pigeons! I runned at them and they flied away!" He is so thrilled with his work and with that, he sees another quarry and immediately turns on his heel to resume his very important job.

The mum smiles after her mini, pigeon terroriser and then at her smaller charge in the buggy beside her.

"Beautiful baby," I say as our eyes meet.

"Thanks so much, she is very good, a great sleeper and eater, but I think that I am more relaxed this time round, and I think they know if you are stressed." She rocks the buggy a little as the baby starts to stir.

"Is it just the two you have?" I ask.

"No, she's my third. The older two are both boys and I always wanted a little girl. I know it's wrong now to want the pink things, but I have to confess I love getting her little bits and pieces." She leans forward conspiratorially, "Do you know on my first I was almost sterilising myself! I was so stressed about germs, on the second I was lucky to get bottles in the steriliser for a few minutes and sure for her, all her stuff goes in the dishwasher and she is as healthy as a horse!"

We chat and laugh together in the early afternoon sun, until the terror of the pigeons has run the feet off himself and it is time for my café companion to take her leave and head home. I am reminded of how easy it is to talk to people here and how it seems as though there are less barriers to conversation; more acceptance that people will just start to talk and be happy to listen. My latte is finished, and the delicious scone consumed. I scatter the crumbs for the lingering pigeons who have remained unperturbed by the big chase. I head back over to the door of the café and call a brief goodbye to Mick. He returns my farewell with a brief wave as he is creating another coffee creation behind the machine.

As I exit the park, I notice a person in “Kecks” whom I recognise, laying down on the pavement, with a small paper cup on the ground, in front of his prostrate form. I look a little closer and see the word “Help” on the cup. I do not have any change in my pocket and really do not want to disturb the sleeping figure of Jim. The convenience store is just up the road and as luck would have it, I see Kiera working inside.

“Excuse me,” I say.

“Yes? Oh, it’s yourself,” she says. “You were in last night, somewhere near Luton?”

“Well not quite, but close enough,” I reply. It really does not matter where exactly I came from, not at this moment in time and in this place. “I have a question,” I Say. “That scruffy looking man that was in the shop last night, do you know anything about him?”

Kiera takes a moment; I can see she is trying to think exactly when I had been in and to whom I was referring.

“You asked him to pull his trousers up,” I say, thinking more specifics might help.

Again, she is thinking. It occurs to me that maybe men with gravity-challenged pants may not be so unusual here, and what must this poor girl have to marshal daily? Then, a flash of recognition.

"Jim!" she exclaims, "Yes Jim is a bit of a sad case really. I don't know a lot about him, but I think he has always lived around here. He has a bit of a problem with the drink and as a result seems to drift in and out of hostels and such. He is a decent enough fella when he is sober, but that seems to be less and less frequent in recent times. Sad really."

"Well, he is outside laying on the pavement, is there anything I could get for him that isn't booze?" I ask.

"He loves cheese and coleslaw sandwiches and is very partial to a bar of milk chocolate," Kiera replies. "Probably would be no harm to get some water and maybe a couple of bottles of minerals; but listen to me adding to your shopping list and me not knowing how much you want to spend! The cheek of me!" she laughs.

"Look get all those bits and pop them in a bag, would you?" I say. "It is awful to see someone so far down on their luck. I know it is not really the answer, but I guess it is only day one here for me; I will give Jim some thought."

Kiera bags the items and I settle up with her. I lift the drinks and food off the counter and walk back to the sleeping figure of Jim. I gingerly place the bag next to him and rustle the bag a little to let him know something is there. He opens one rheumy eye, looks at the bag and mutters, "Thanks a million, missus. He pulls the bag and its contents into his arms and promptly falls back asleep. I thoughtfully walk back to Grove House to make my grocery list for my "big shop." The local supermarket is calling me, and who am I to deny the pull of urban hunter gathering! I make a list of what I need for my lunches and dinners. I remind myself that in addition to food, I will need to get cleaning products and not to forget essentials like toilet roll; now that would be an oversight!

Chapter 5

I am not normally one to make a big deal out of shopping, in fact it would be safe to say I am not a fan at all. For the past number of months, it has only been for me and that's the way it will be for the foreseeable future. However, this is another adventure for me. Every opportunity to see the day to day in another country, who would not be excited about that?

Despite it being early days I feel as though I am knitting in here and even a trip to do the shopping is just another way to get a feel for my new home. I once heard my aunt say to me that the rest of the world has six degrees of separation, but in Ireland you are lucky if you get to three degrees without someone piping up that their brother's girlfriend's sister knows someone who knows you from school. This always made me laugh when I was younger and coming to Ireland on holiday. It was never long before dad found some common acquaintance with a stranger he met. That is one of the reasons why I feel this is a great place to be, to just reconnect with the culture my dad grew up with, the familiar unfamiliar.

In order to get the shopping I need, I have to take my car with me and navigate the roads again, but I get over myself, take my bags for life and head towards the nearest store. It feels strange to rediscover how roomy the car is after the laden, lengthy journey of the past days. The Golf seems suddenly palatial, and I turn the radio on and find an 80's music station. I hum along to myself as I head down the road following the instructions issued by my trusty phone, but today with the benefit of a good night's sleep rather than at the end of a long journey, and I respond to the automated voice telling me to "take the next left." Fortunately for me, it is still too early for homeward bound commuter traffic and the short journey is not impeded by stopping and starting. I lower the windows and enjoy the breeze, as late summer sunshine warms the car and gives a continental feel to the North Circular Road. I can see groups of small black flies randomly picking jagged flight paths over the hedges at the side of the road.

The familiar supermarket logo comes into view, and I turn into the carpark. There are very few cars lining the parking bays. Once out of the car, I head towards the lines of shopping trolleys. I check to see if I have change. I have a few one-euro coins in my purse. As I take one to place it in the unlocking mechanism of the trolley, I notice the sticker. Just my luck; it is of course two euro slot. What to do? I hear steps behind me and a man clearing his throat. I know I am in the way and as I turn to apologise I see an man standing behind me. He is taller than me, around 5 feet 10 inches and is slim, other than a small paunch of tummy. His clothing is neat and tidy, and I notice his very well-polished shoes. He has the air of someone who has always looked after himself and taken time over his clothes, even for the supermarket shop.

"Are you alright there missus?" he asks.

"Sorry," I say, "I'm afraid that I don't have a blasted two-euro coin, I have a few one euro, but they are of no use here."

"No, that's true," the man replies, "of course you could see if you could find someone who might exchange your euros for one of those two-euro coins, that might be an idea."

I cannot decide if he is saying this because he may be my knight in shining armour or because he is just sarcastic and merely wants me to get out of the way so that he can go about his business. A pregnant pause. I think that if I leave a silence between us, then he will either come up with a solution or tell me to shove out of the way.

The gap of reply is like drought in the conversation and is painful even though it is only momentary. I do not know what the etiquette is, do I ask if he has the correct change, or do I wait for him to offer?

I watch him slowly take out a coin wallet from his jacket pocket. He opens the wallet, looks in and surveys the contents. He carefully tips out the contents of the wallet and I see a few coins fall into his left hand. He picks out two and I can see things are looking up.

"Think that this is what you are looking for," he says.

I am a little surprised to see him reach out his hand to retrieve the two one-euro coins from me, before handing over the shopping-trolley-releasing two-euro coin. So surprised in fact, that I just participate in this transaction without thought.

"Thank you so much," I say, "that's very good of you, I have only just moved over and had assumed that all trolleys would take one-euro coins. I have always had those token things before, but they are the wrong size for here."

I know that I am still in his way and at this stage I am rambling. Finally, the money is in the slot, the trolley released, another apology and thank you uttered, and I am finally out of the way.

I walk past a disinterested security guard, scrutinising his phone screen. I am not sure how much he is actively observing, but maybe if there is an emergency, I will see him leap into action; unlikely as that may seem in his current state of preoccupation.

The thing about discount supermarkets is that they have perfected the art of echoing the product names used by big brands, but with subtle differences, enough to be evocative for shoppers but distanced sufficiently to avoid lawsuits. I commence my shop purchasing "Wheat Bikkies" and "Honey Loopy Hoops" (just for a treat at the weekend!). The shopping list of not-quite-the-real-things continues, packaging hinting at the contents being distant relatives of branded cousins. I make sure to stock up on my "five a day" fruit and veg and everything here looks fresh and appetising. Apples, bananas, grapes, lettuce, tomatoes are all put into the trolley which is starting to look like a Frida Kahlo painting in a riot of organic colour.

I manage to sidestep the central aisles offering all manner of quite frankly, inexplicable neighbours on the shelves. I stand, trying to work out the connection between the special offer on cat litter and the play garage sitting next to power hoses, but I believe that the power of the central aisles is that they bring out the bargain hunter in the most resistant of customers.

However, I am not beguiled by what is on offer (especially as I don't have a cat, a small child or a patio that needs hosing), and feel rather pleased with myself for not falling under the spell of the offers of the week.

I make my way to the bank of tills. In my experience, this is always something of a lottery as the lights can change colour on a till at the drop of a hat. A till can be open and then closed and then declared re-opened in the course of a few moments, you must be really on your toes to keep up with the abrupt changes. I choose a lane that looks promising and prepare to have my dreams shattered if that till is closed. The lady in front of me has piled the conveyor belt high with her food shopping. She has made the schoolgirl error of standing fizzy drinks bottles upright and as the conveyor moves forward two of the bottles fall over and one then drops on the floor. Something to look forward to when the lid is opened.

There is an art to a checkout and I pride myself on being something of an expert. Firstly, the checkout operators are freakishly fast at their jobs. If there was an Olympic category for product scanning, I think that the staff in these shops would sweep the board with the medals. Secondly, you must be prepared to get your goods into bags as soon as you can. There is of course, what I like to think of as the realm of the less-savvy customers, the line of 'packing' shelves after the tills, but to my mind it is about being totally in the zone. I fold down my bags for life to create a rigid reinforcement to each bag. I then organise them in the trolley with an extra bag hanging on the back of the trolley for bread and eggs (or the squishy stuff as I like to think of it). It is then the allocation across the bags ready to receive fruit and veg, ambient and frozen and then another for cans and jars. I work quickly to get the shopping packed as quickly as it is scanned. I refuse to be relegated to the packing shelf section, no not today, I will be victorious and complete the loading of the bags with time to spare for payment and even a cheery thank you to my checkout adversary. This is all going very well, and I feel confident in the outcome, until a carton splits and the conveyor is coated in strawberry yoghurt. The checkout equivalent of a stewards' enquiry follows, with a replacement sought and everything wiped down. So near and yet so far. I will have to make sure that the next time I come in that I will double check for squashed dairy goods! All's well that ends well and I am finally exiting the store with purchases made and the prospect of a full fridge and cupboards for the week.

On my way back to Grove House I see Jim sitting on a garden wall watching the world go by whilst once again he give the impression of being stuck in time. He speaks,

"Can you spare me some change missus?" His voice is gravelly, and I can smell the stale sweat from his clothing.

"Hello, you're Jim, aren't you?" I reply.

He looks slightly confused and taken aback that I neither said that I do not have any money nor handed cash over without comment.

"Ermmmm yes that's me, do I know you?" A flash of worry and confusion on his face and I can see that he is not sure what to do next.

"We sort of bumped into each other the other evening in the shop down the road. You probably don't remember; I was being served after you. Nice to meet you properly Jim, my name is Angie." I open my purse, find some change and go to hand it to him. I notice he is reluctant to take it, but slowly reaches forward.

"Very kind of you, I'm sure. God Bless you," I realise that this may be the first time he has been properly 'seen' today and acknowledged by his name. What an existence, when there is no affirmation of your given name or of you as a human being? It really is the small things in life that that make a difference.

Chapter 6

I wake up at 5.45 am and strain to listen for Ursula tripping the light fantastic upstairs... no not this morning there is no syncopated sashaying, maybe it is Pilates today rather than the salsa she loves so much. I get up and grab a quick breakfast and make my lunch of a wholemeal salad sandwich ready to take in to work on my first day. I also retrieve the tin of biscuits I had purchased the day before; the contents a wonderful mix of bourbon creams, shortbread, garibaldi and pink wafers, what more could a girl want? My mouth waters and I realise that my waistline will not weather the storm of the contents of the tin if I keep them at home. I decide that it will be a nice gesture to my new colleagues at work if I take the biscuits in to share, (in my experience sweet things have a wonderful way of breaking down barriers, a shared sugar rush is generally well regarded).

I grab the final few personal items I am going to take with me. A small jar of decaffeinated coffee (I confess I am mainly a tea drinker but sometimes just fancy a coffee), a pack of sweetener and my own mug with a picture of honeysuckle, my birth flower. I am dressed in my uniform of navy trousers and a light blue cotton tunic as specified in my letter of appointment. The tunic is crisp with sharp folds down the short sleeves. I admire the finished look in the mirror. This is the tunic of a person who means to put her best foot forward. I feel that I will be able to do just that in my new black runners purchased for their beautiful spongey sole. If I have learned anything in life then it is, if you are on your feet all day, it is a lot easier if memory foam intercedes between your feet and the floor! It is still not easy though and I know that it will take a while to get back into the swing of a normal working day; even after a little break. Lots of new things to learn as well, with health and safety procedures, medications, names...! I am dreadful at learning lots of new names at the same time! I think that my brain is just not wired to recall who is who. I once tried one of those natty memory techniques which suggested that you associated the name with an object as well as the person's face. The only trouble was when I tried, I was thinking about plates, plants, in fact anything except the name! As this is the case, and I know my limitations when planning to take on a whole staff and resident list on board in one go, I have a small notebook with me that I can list names along with important snippets about each person that will help me to get names set in my head quicker. I know this may sound a bit weird, but it has got me out of a few sticky situations in the past.

Everything is packed and I am ready to go. One last check that the flat is clean, tidy and appliances switched off. Rucksack over shoulder and I am off. I have the returning sense of excitement and trepidation as I lock the door behind me. I hear the quiet click of the door catch opposite and glance to see Sinead looking out through the crack.

"Hi Sinead!" I call. "Beautiful morning to be heading out, it's my first day at work down the road."

Nothing came the reply. "Are you heading out yourself today?" I figure it may be worth pursuing the conversation, despite it being very one- sided at this point.

A quiet, "No, I don't do that," is the response. I am puzzled. Does not do what? Go out? I am stumped as to what to say next. I know I have a couple of minutes before I have to be off, but it sounds as though this girl living opposite me, may have a real concern about going into the outside world.

"Would you like me to bring you anything home later then?" I do not really know why I am even asking that question. I have only just arrived on the scene, why on earth would I be able to do anything? I am sure she has all her living needs covered, whether it involves leaving her flat or not.

"No...." a hesitation, "But thanks, that is very nice of you." The words are followed by the catch on the door and again she is gone. I think it is a step, albeit tiny step, in the right direction.

I head down the stairs and they creak slightly as my feet hit each riser. Down and out into the morning. The trees show that the summer is getting old, their summer lushness growing tired in the advancing year. The leaves are still clinging to their branches, but a few are starting to change hue from their summer green to flashes of gold, soon to turn copper and drop from their lofty bows. I hear the green door click as it closes behind me, a breeze ruffles my fringe, fresh and clean at this early hour of the morning. I am positive that this will be a good day and walk out through the gate and towards my new job. This is a morning full of the possibility of the new.

I walk purposefully down the road to The Beeches. I observe the departures from the houses along the road, other purposeful striders heading for work and slightly slower paces marshalling their children towards creches and schools. The parents toting multi-coloured mini rucksacks, scooters, favourite toys and precious items for their young charges. Occasionally the little ones stopping to marvel at a "creature" or a fascinating stone or leaf. The world is filled with wonder to small eyes but youthful wonder and deadlines are not happy partners, and I can see a couple of the parents becoming exasperated with the slow pace.

My walk takes twenty minutes before I arrive at the front door of The Beeches. The manager asked me to arrive slightly later than usual this morning for her to organise her own work before she starts my first day orientation. Six o'clock is going to be my usual time, the crack of sparrows, lucky that I am a morning person!

The building is double fronted, not dissimilar in style to Grove House. It is set slightly further back from the road than Grove House. The polished brass plate at the front gate announces, "The Beeches Residential Care Home." The dark tarmac of the driveway is a smooth and perfect track to the front of the building. It is edged with red stone sets, and I cannot see a single weed. Close to the front entrance, there are two bays marked out; one with a disabled wheelchair sign painted in white and the other with the words "Ambulances only." There is a sign directing to parking at the rear of the building for staff that require it and for visitors.

The Japanese anemones in the front border are in full bloom, with stems reaching upwards to hip height, their magenta flowers swaying slightly in the whisper of the air. The bay windows of the day room on the ground floor curve outwards, almost reaching to the flowers, inviting them to come in and show their beautiful blooms to the residents in the home.

I buzz the bell at the front door and a slightly tinny voice responds. Leaning into the speaker I state my name and that I am a new starter today. Buzz. The door releases and I walk in to a second interior door, the glass criss-crossed with an inner wire that glints slightly in the light.

Another buzz and I walk through to stand outside the administration office.

The wide hallway has white walls with signup sheets for line dancing, painting, macrame, hairdressing, chiropody, and all manner of services. This is a hub of things going on! Telephones are ringing, hushed voices talking. The smells of the home are a combination of polish, antiseptic, coffee and breakfast - a heady combination. Tapping on the white panelled office door I peek around to see two ladies inside. Both wear the same uniform as me.

The lady closest to the door looks up. Her eyes are the thing I first notice, they are blue with a faint tinge of grey. They have a hint of the promise of a good sense of humour and the faint lines at the corners of her eyes and at the edges of her mouth tell me that this is a lady who approaches life with laughter in her heart. Her name badge says “Maureen” and she has drawn a smiley face after it. Maureen has her dark hair drawn back into a ponytail fastened with a bright canary yellow scrunchie. She tucks a wayward strand behind her ear and smiles.

“Welcome Angie,” she says, “I think that you have brought the weather with you on your first day! What a beautiful morning!” She turns and speaks to the other lady

“Niamh, this is Angie,” Niamh raises a finger, she’s on the phone and listening attentively. I can hear a faint lilt of muzak from the phone. At least she is not actually talking to a person and Maureen takes no notice of this indication to pause.

“Niamh,” pointing at me, “this is Angie, her first day today, she has just moved over from England.....Niamh!”

Niamh lets out a “Humph,” as she replaces the phone in its cradle. I have no idea what she has been holding for, but this abrupt interruption clearly makes her unhappy as she turns to look at me. She has auburn hair with a creamy complexion that does not look as though it would fare well in anything other than the Irish climate.

Her eyes are brown, and her manner suggests that she is not best friends with Maureen. Niamh nods and I say a brief "Hello" and immediately Maureen whisks me from the office to take me to the staffroom where I will find my locker.

"Niamh is grand, a bit of a stickler for the rules though so just mind that you are clear on what is what. I'm sure that you will get to know the routine with no problem. You will be grand, I have a schedule of the activities you will need to be aware of, it will be second nature in no time at all!" This is all uttered quickly whilst walking briskly to the staff room.

The staffroom is bright, the morning sunlight coming though fanlight windows and strip lighting playing a supporting role this morning. The walls are a zesty shade of lemon lined with pale grey lockers on one side, a fridge and low cabinets on the other. The counter is neat and there are several pastel-lidded plastic boxes containing crackers, fruit and biscuits (grapes seem to be particularly popular gauging the round green silhouettes hinting through the opaque boxes), each one announcing their unseen owners by handwritten labels. There is a large whiteboard on the wall with a grid of room numbers and resident names. Adjacent to the whiteboard is the large cork board that has several brightly coloured thank you cards attached by red drawing pins. A couple of the cards have faded slightly where the sun has hit them and taken back some of their colour. In the middle of the room there are two small square tables with chairs tucked underneath. It is ordered, it is very clean, and I have a feeling that it will not take long to settle in. Two of the other carers on shift today come in. Maureen introduces me to them. Martina and Camilla smile their welcomes and head back out quickly to attend to their mornings duties.

"You will have to set a code on your locker, we tried to go with padlocks but then some of the carers were losing keys and it all became a bit of a nightmare to tell you the truth so now we go with the combinations, you know like on a suitcase?" Maureen points to the locker she is allocating to me.

I take out my lunch box and throw my rucksack into the locker, set a combination, and place my lunch into the fridge that is in the corner of the staff room. Behind me the kettle has reached its boiling point and Maureen asks, "Tea or coffee?"

"Tea please," I reply, "just a drop of milk, thank you."

The mugs of tea are placed on one of the tables. Once I settle on the chair opposite her Maureen commences,

"There are fifteen members of staff here Angie and we cover 20 residents in total," she points behind her to the white board with a grid of names.

"We have a two-weekly roster as I outlined in your letter of offer, the shifts are 12 hours and we do try to accommodate preferences as much as possible, some of the girls have young families and actually prefer working night shifts whilst their mums mind their kids for them. We find it all balances out between members of staff and how they prefer to work. Of course, there are times when it is all-hands-on-deck, but those times are few and far between to be honest with you."

I nod, all that makes sense to me. I know that I would prefer the daytime shift because it will give me more of a chance to get to know the residents and be in step with other people outside work, but in truth nights are fine too. It is great to have found a job so local to where I live and where I can start immediately. Fingers crossed I will not be called too quickly for the night shift.

"The most important thing here Angie is we offer residential care. We really pride ourselves on getting to know each resident and their family and friends. It is through us knowing each person that it makes it possible for us to make them more comfortable. The decision to come into a residential home has not been an easy one for some of our clients and it is our job to help that transition," Maureen takes a sip of her tea.

"We encourage all staff to share information with each other so that even if one of us only spends a few minutes with one of the residents during the course of the day, the others can fill in the gaps and we have a complete picture of the person."

This is such a good idea. I love the way the team are encouraged to work together in this way. I had been very privileged to have had such a depth of understanding about my own aunt when I cared for her. She had been part of my story all my life and I knew all her likes, dislikes and little foibles that made her herself. This seems to be the next best thing.

"We have a resident of the day every day. We focus on discussing an individual each day and share the details that add to the story of the resident. This makes such a difference in making each person feel settled. Of course, this is all in addition to the handover briefings after each shift. If there are any particular comments make a note on the whiteboard to raise."

The manual for The Beeches is held in a red A4 folder. Each section has a pastel divider labelled with headings such as deliveries, medication, laundry, room inventory lists, food and food intolerances, Garda vetting forms. A whole raft of information designed to make this place work and to put the care and safety of the residents at the heart of the job. It all seems straightforward, and I know what my bedtime reading will be when Maureen hands me the folder to peruse at my leisure.

Maureen stands up and lets me know that it is the time to start learning "on the job."

This will be a morning of visiting residents, saying my hellos, lots of, "Yes, I am from England, just moved over a few days ago, but my dad was Irish, and I have visited many times."

The residents are mainly women as is the case in most residential homes. The Beeches does not have the facilities to cater for high dependency elders. I keep an eye out for Mick's mam Breda. Finally, I alight upon her room as I am taking in her morning tea and biscuits. I know for sure that it is Breda because there is a framed photograph next to her bed of Leopold Bloom sporting a bright red Christmas jumper decorated with knitted holly and looking thoroughly miserable.

"Good morning," I greet her as I place the tea and biscuits next to her on a side table in her room. Breda's room is on the ground floor, and it is the policy of the home that residents can have their own pictures and keepsakes in their rooms to make them as homely as possible. Breda has a brightly coloured crocheted blanket over her bed, swirls of blue, green, lemons and white cascading across the design showing the complex movements the crochet needle had taken to master the yarn. The intricate stitches and details are mesmerising; someone took a long time to produce this wonderful piece of work.

Breda looks towards me and an expression of puzzlement flashes across her wrinkled face.

"You're new," she states, "Haven't seen you before, what's your name when it's at home then?"

I begin to get a sense of why Leopold Bloom has a more than slightly prickly exterior. He had not licked his feisty attitude off the stones, as my aunt would have said.

"Hello Breda, my name is Angie, yep I am new, first day today and just getting the chance to get to know everyone," I reply.

"It would fit you better to bring some decent biscuits," Breda surveys the digestives on the plate next to her cup of tea with disdain. "I am sick of these things," she continues, "You'd think with the money they are charging here there would at least be the occasional chocolate hobnob, but no it's feckin' digestives every day." She glances at me to see if I am offended by her language. I have the distinct impression that Breda takes quite a lot of joy out of shocking people, but I have been well prepared for profanity by my aunt who was known to swear like a trooper, a situation that only got worse as her health deteriorated. I am more than equal to anything that Breda can throw at me!

“Do you have a favourite biscuit Breda?” I ask.

“At this point I’d eat anything other than these bleedin’ things!” she points her sinewy fingers towards the hateful digestives with a look of profound disgust on her face.

“I might be able to help you out with that little problem,” I say as I turn to leave her room and head back to my locker. I had forgotten to leave the biscuits out on the counter in the staff room and instead, lift one of each kind of biscuit, slip them into my tunic pocket and quickly return to Breda’s room.

I can tell that she is quite surprised to see me again so quickly.

“What do you want?” This woman clearly has no expertise in the field of diplomacy or social niceties. I place the biscuits on the plate next to the digestives. The chocolate, the rich buttery colour of the shortbread and the pink wafers look like a veritable explosion of colour compared to the drab workaday digestives. The expression on Breda’s face changes from a scowl, to disbelief, to delight. Each emotion fleeting, other than the joy of taking in what she is seeing.

"For me?" She looks up hopefully and reaches out for the pink wafer first. It is a layered rectangle of sugary sweetness. Pink and perfect in her gnarled hand. She raises it to her lips and takes the smallest of nibbles. This is biscuit heaven. She is elevated to a place of happiness, and I can see a shadow of her younger self, as she lets down the cynical guard she presents to the world now. After the last crumb has been savoured and this chapter of biscuit heaven is concluded, she smiles. An actual smile with no snideness and no smart comment.

"That was only delicious," she says, "what did you say your name is again?"

"Angie, nice to meet you Breda," I reply. "I am living in the same place as your son Mick, I met him the other day."

"But how would you know about Mick and me being related?" she asks and immediately I get a sense of the prickly exterior being reinstated.

I nod towards the photograph of Leopold Bloom.

"You met my Leo?" Again her face lights up and I see a woman who is brusque on the outside but at the thought of her Yorkshire Terrier she is a softy.

"Oh yes and I met Leo too!" I laugh, "Mick had him in a high visibility jacket, Leo cuts quite a dash!"

"Mick has been very good to me," she replies, "I really was not able to cope at home and with Mick running the café there was no way he was able to take the time off work to run all the messages and look after me. He has been so good to take Leo in, I do not know what would have become of him otherwise. Don't get me wrong, I know that Leo is a little gobshite, but he's my little gobshite and sure doesn't that make all the difference?"

"Do you get to see much of Leo, Breda?" I ask.

"As much as Mick's work hours allow," she replies. "That one Niamh will not allow Leo into the home on account of the fact that the last time he was in, the little beggar cocked his leg all over Mrs Brennan in the day room and Niamh says that he is a health risk to the residents now. If he had behaved himself, he may have been allowed in the garden, but he's such a little devil that he tried to snap at Niamh when she went to remove him and she banned him from here altogether."

I stifle a giggle. I had met Mrs Brennan earlier on my introductions and she seemed like a lovely woman. The idea of Leo violating her in that way tickles my slightly twisted sense of humour. Niamh is probably right; Leo maybe is not suited to be one of those "visiting" type dogs who help residents to be comforted. He is more of a "Gobshite" dog, to quote Breda, who would pee on you as soon as look at you. Maybe Niamh has the right idea as I must confess, I do not fancy wiping Leo's accidents off the legs of any of the residents! At the same time, it is a bit sad really, I will have to think of a way around this.

"Is there anything else I can get for you Breda?" I ask.

"Not at all Angie," she says, "sure what more could a woman want, you have made my morning with the bikkies!"

As I leave her room, I see one of my colleagues, Martina, escorting one of the residents down the corridor. Martina smiles as she sees me.

"Here Moira, have you met Angie yet? She is new here and started earlier today,"

Moira looks slightly confused as she turns to face me. She has a lovely face, and I am sure that she was quite the looker when she was younger. Her blouse and cardigan are peach which create a warm reflection on her complexion. I can see that she is trying to place me but failing. I recall from the staff room white board that the words "walks with purpose" were next to Moira's name on the grid. This lovely lady is in the early stages of dementia and wanders through the home.

"Here we are Moira," Martina says, "Here we are back at your room, we will just head back in for a wee moment and get you sorted out," Martina smiles at me and gently guides Moira into her room. I watch the two women as they walk together, the carer and the cared for. I am sure that this is not what Moira envisaged for herself when she was younger. None of us know what is around the corner and this makes me realise that my new neighbour Ursula is absolutely right with her neon and get out into the world attitude. I am going to take a leaf out of her book, who knows, it could be salsa next!

The Beeches diary is a busy one and each day goes past quickly. Today all the residents are invited to head into the large day room at 11.30 am. A line dancing class is the activity of the day led by a wonderfully cheery lady called Carol. She stands at the front of the room wearing a red neckerchief and beautifully decorated black leather cowboy boots. Her hair is a rich copper tone and styled in waves. Her enthusiasm is contagious as she sets up for the session. She has hellos and how are you for everyone and greets everyone with a cheery smile. She coaxes the residents to get involved in the class with promises of cheery fun and the rallying comment, "Movement is Life!"

Carol's encouragement is met with a mix of responses. Ten of the twenty residents get up from their armchairs.

Three of the ladies are even wearing rather jaunty chiffon neck scarves. They form two horizontal lines of five standing in front of Carol. She proceeds to take them through some breathing and very gentle stretching exercise to prepare them for their dancing. Carol wears a microphone linked to a speaker, a necessary piece of kit for our less well of hearing residents. Exercises complete the dancing begins. The opening "warm up tune" appears to be a favourite with the dancers and the class begins.

Carol's instructions speak over the music, "Forward, two, three, four, back two, three, four," and so on.

The dancers go through their moves, while the remainder either watch or, in the case of three of the residents, have a little nap. The music selection is primarily country music as you would expect.

It is fair to say that some of the dancers demonstrate more rhythm than others, but the common theme are the smiles on their faces as they turn and face the different walls during the dances. The music and the opportunity to dance is invaluable to them all and even the residents sitting down and watching are tapping their feet and clapping. Just joyous! Camilla grabs the hands of one of the seated ladies, June I think her name is, and the two of them "dance" with Camilla standing and June in her armchair. June laughs and sings along when she hears a modern version of her favourite song.

As Carol is packing up after the line dancing, I see our dancers going over to her and giving her a little hug. She has a few words with them all and is clearly very attached to each and every one of her dancing troupe. Camilla comes over and stands next to me.

"Carol is such a tonic! She really does bring a bit of life into the place, her own mum passed about a year ago and was a big fan of music so this is Carol's way of being involved and doing something in the memory of her lovely mum." Camilla does a little shimmy and then bumps her hip against mine as she heads back to June who is having problems getting up from her seat.

"Here I am June my lovely, hold on there and we will get you sorted in no time!" Camilla supports June as she gets out of her chair, a team effort that ends successfully.

After Carol has finished her packing up, she has a quick scan to see that she has everything and calls out a cheery, "See you all next week, keep dancing!"

The lift that this half an hour of music and movement has given to the dancers and their audience is almost tangible and reinforces to me the way the home tries to bring fun through activities.

The rest of my shift involves serving residents' lunches, medication rounds, some family visitors, teatime and finally the team debrief at the end of the shift. Somehow, I manage to grab my own sandwich in the middle of all the activity and the brief sit down is very welcome.

We gather in the staff room to talk through our day and to record anything that may be of help to the team working the night shift. All seems well. Martina does mention that Moira is a bit more confused than usual and that we should all keep an eye out to make sure that she does not wander and put herself in danger.

I gather my rucksack and prepare to leave for the day. I am tired and happy. Another big tick in the box. I head out into the evening. The remnants of the late summer day are still warming the footpaths and the air is moted with specs of dust, seemingly suspended on invisible lines until they suddenly veer left or right. I begin my walk back towards Grove House amazingly feeling as though I am floating, despite the day on my feet, let's hear it for memory foam insoles!

Arriving home, I do not see any of the other residents, but there are faint mutterings from televisions and radios that let me know that I am not alone in the building. I do not feel alone. I have always been quite comfortable with my own company and truth be told, I have always enjoyed sojourns from people, a chance to just be and recharge. I get out my affirmation cards; as I turn the first one over, I blink my eyes shut then peer, "The best is yet to come!" Well, that fills me with the little boost I need. There is a knock at the door. Mick stands outside with Leo in his arms, Leo is wearing a rather fetching orange tutu under his high vis jacket. I decide discretion is the better part of valour and say nothing.

"I was wondering if you had seen Mam today?" Mick enquires. "The café was really busy, and I didn't get a chance to get down to her. I thought what with today being your first day that you may've seen her?"

I thought of his feisty mam with her craving for less bland biscuits and smiled. "Yep, met your mum. She's a real character and we had a great chat, one thing that is obvious is that she thinks the world of you," I replied. Mick smiles.

"That she is! A tough old boot, I mean that in the nicest way! Did she say if she needed anything?" Mick enquires, "I will try to get in to see her tomorrow if the café isn't too busy in the afternoon.

"Fancy biscuits," I say. "She seems to be a bit anti the regular digestives on offer, so definitely a fancier biscuit than the humble digestive!"

“She’s always had a fierce sweet tooth,” Mick grins. His expression is soft and there are faint laughter lines around his eyes. I can see the suggestion of Breda’s features on her son’s face. The definition of their cheeks and the shape of their lips are identical, there’s no mistaking that he is her son.

“There were always loads of biscuits and sweet treats in the house as I was growing up, she never lost it to this day! Right, that’s my instruction so, biscuits it is! Thanks Angie.”

I recall Leo’s misdemeanour with Mrs Brennan, “I’ve heard why this little fella is not allowed in The Beeches as well! He certainly blotted his copy book with his ‘accident.’”

Mick grins, “That wasn’t even the half of it Angie! I think that he may have been forgiven for having an accident, but the final nail in the coffin was the day of the macrame demonstration, now that was really what caused the problem!”

I am intrigued, Breda had not mentioned this. “What happened that day?” I ask.

“Well, most of the residents and staff had been taken into the day room and a few of us relatives were invited to join them. I managed to get time from the café and took this little bugger with me. In truth, he was well behaved but, what no one noticed, was him falling asleep under Niamh's chair. About five minutes into the demonstration, Leo started letting out the almightiest farts and of course no one could see him. This went on for the whole demonstration and everyone thought that it was Niamh! Now that is the real reason, he is now persona non grata at the home!"

I picture the scene. Niamh doing her best to be dignified in front of the other staff and each and every one of them thinking that she was giving off this awful stench. That must have been so very embarrassing for her, but oh my goodness so funny to listen to. No wonder Leo is not allowed in The Beeches!

Mick nods his farewell and heads back down the stairs, with Leo snuggled up like a small furry package in his arms.

I relax with one last cup of milky tea with the window open, letting in the evening sounds of the city traffic as it abates after the commuters are safely back home, awaiting their journeys of the following days. I sip my tea and strain to hear the faint noises of the zoo animals settling for the night and peace.

Chapter 7

A month into my new job. The flat is working out well and I am beginning to really feel at home. I easily fall into the routine of the walk to work, with every day offering new things to observe along the way. My earlier starts means that I am sharing the pavements with the commuters heading to their jobs rather than those on school runs. I miss the young students, often dawdling and observing things only the young with their youthful sense of amazement see. The chatter of discovery made me look again at things that familiarity often renders invisible.

However, the lights are on in the upstairs of the houses as people are getting ready for their days. I wear my EarPods and listen to the radio as I walk along. I love listening to the radio early in the morning, it gives me a sense of what's what here. Even though it is a national radio station, there is an engaging sense of place in the way the stories are covered. A quintessential sense of being part of this city and this country. The news bulletins cover BREXIT and broader brushes across the globe with stories of Trumpian USA and unrest in the Middle East. Domestic politics and policies are discussed as the parties vie for support in what will soon be an election year. My mornings are filled with the world through the airwaves.

The work days have a regular rhythm. Morning calls, breakfasts, activities, coffee, lunches, afternoon tea and then dinner. All the food, denture and delicate palate friendly. A persistent aroma of cooking from the kitchens and a faint scent of bleach and polish that permeates the rest of the building act as a reminder of the nature of The Beeches.

The activities create a tempo of life here with the regular visitors and events creating a reassuringly familiar framework. I love the sense of expectation on the days when the bingo or the dancing burst into the residents' sitting room. The activity co-ordinators bring a piece of the outside world into the four walls with them, as if their clothes bear tiny hooks like teasels grasping and catching pieces of the former lives and routines of our residents. The residents' removal from their old day to day lives can lead to commentaries on a loop. The days can be very repetitive without visits and distractions. The visits, entertainment and activities alleviate the absence of trips out to the shops and the other trappings of their younger lives. I do not think that the visitors and activity co-ordinators are entirely aware of the fragments of joy they carry here with them, why would they? Their experience of here is that the rays of sunlight are always present in the room when they arrive. They do not feel the charge of expectation that occurs before they cross the threshold and that is what makes the value of the volunteers so precious.

I like my colleagues; we are a band of carers from many backgrounds and life experiences, and we are here with a common purpose. Maureen is kind and endeavours to include me in staff room chats with the other members of staff. I appreciate that and it is not too long that I begin to feel more than the new girl. I feel that the mix of circumstances and hopes brings a pleasant richness to our breaktime conversations. Niamh is harder to work out however, despite her tetchiness, she is fine if you follow the rules and do not cause her any extra stress or hassle. The other girls are very likeable, and their company and good humour make the days pass quickly, even when a particular day is challenging.

I think that the hardest things to manage on an emotional level are our two residents with early-stage dementia. They are both beautiful and gentle souls but every day they live a bit less with the rest of the residents. It seems that they are fading from themselves over a short period of time, like the reverse of the way photographs used to be developed before everything became digital. Moira's family do visit regularly, but I see their bags of photo albums and their eyes watery as they leave for the memories they have tried to rekindle without success. It is not easy to see a loved one steadily slipping from the gossamer threads of everyone else's reality. Moira loves a bit of Frank Sinatra and I often hear lilts of "My Way" coming from her room as my colleagues try to help her recapture some element of herself and we all comment that 'Ol Blue Eyes does put a twinkle back into her unengaged expression. Moira has two favourite possessions that now accompany her everywhere – her blue towel and her beaded glasses case. Another resident Pauline also struggles significantly with her memory. Her diagnosis is not as advanced as Moira's and it is very difficult to watch her struggling with a half-known realisation that this is happening to her. Pauline's family do not live close by, and their visits are quite sporadic, I have not seen them visit since I started working here and I know that she is already forgetting them when I ask who feature in the photographs in her room. I truly hope that they get the opportunity to see her while she still has some capacity to know who they are, otherwise, they will face two losses.

There is a dramatic contrast between Moira and Pauline and the three residents who are friends and have known each other before they moved into The Beeches. Mary, Gloria and Betty have been pals for years and are involved in all manner of societies and charities together. Gloria is an out and out bon viveur with a fierce sense of humour. Mary regales all the staff and residents with hilarious stories from her youth and loves a good singsong. Betty is also a singer, and it is obvious that she had been an absolute stunner in her earlier years. The Three Amigos as we call them, embrace all the opportunities for fun and frivolity on the activity days and indeed, lead the laughs at other times. Whenever there is craic to be had in the day room you can be sure that these ladies are at the centre of it. Their favourite song to sing to the other residents is the Doris Day number "Que Sera Sera," harmonised beautifully and taking them on a fast memory train back to the 1950s. The lyrics seem very appropriate for here and now.

It is hard to believe that it is the end of the first month and time has flown by, with routine being my waking hours. Ursula's salsa still syncopates my weekend mornings and occasionally I see a flash of neon as I am heading out to work. She is always flying along, and I still have not had the chance to ask about her prickly cactus community living upstairs. It's funny to think of this vibrant grabber of life surrounding herself with her well-protected succulent housemates and I promise myself to ask her.

A couple of weeks have passed and I have the opportunity, sooner than I could have anticipated, just a few days before Halloween. There are several houses along the road with decorations up, "Trick or Treat" and "Happy Halloween" signs are the flags of the young families and indulgent older residents. Halloween is not really my thing, growing up, the closest thing we got to Halloween celebrations was to bob for apples and to tell ghost stories in the dark. This was quite different, and work was great fun as we decorated the corridors in orange and black streamers and some balloons; Carol's line dancing session that day had included "The Monster Mash" and "Ghostbusters." After the dancing we had cupcakes for all the residents with orange and black icing on top. The Three Amigos have donned witches hats and managed to source green lipstick from somewhere, I think that given half the chance, they would prefer something a bit stronger as a treat than the cups of tea on offer.

As I head in through the front door of Grove House, I see Ursula just in front of me on the stairs and call, "Hi

Ursula! Don't often see you out at this time in the evening."

She turns and smiles, "Well good evening, Angie! Good to see you! I just popped out to get sweets in for the trick or treaters on Halloween. I do not get to see my own grandchildren very often as my daughter lives in America, miss them terribly I do." She looks quite downcast.

I did not know that Ursula had a family, this was really the first time that we had passed anything more than a hello.

"That must be very difficult. I know that I miss my friends over in England, particularly my best friend Paula. I suppose the good thing now is that it is easier to stay in touch, not like a few years ago when you could only write or telephone. Do you talk to them often Ursula?"

"We try to chat every week to ten days; it depends on what they are up to. I don't know, there always seems to be something going on that means that the kids are not free to chat, mind you that probably sounds a bit rich coming from me! I think that you are under the impression that I am never in!"

I am not sure what to say, I do not want to sound rude, but before I can say anything Ursula interjects, "I am only kidding you Angie, your face! A picture it is! Sorry I do not mean to tease!"

I laugh and decide to go for the question that has been tormenting me.

"No worries, Ursula! I hope you don't mind me asking but I have noticed that you have a lot of cactus plants on your windowsills, do you mind me asking why so many?"

A pause.
A smile.
An explanation!

"Angie I was told a long time ago that cacti symbolize patience, endurance and determination. Things I try to bring into my life every day. Over the years I have gifted them to myself if I have ever felt down. Cacti survive every drought but when the rain comes, they rush to absorb every drop and appreciate the true blessing of the falling rain. I love the fact that they store this blessing to keep them going through the dry spells."

"Wow!" I exclaim. "That's just beautiful, I had not thought about cacti like that before, that has completely changed my perception of them!"

Ursula stepped closer, "Angie, I try to be like my cacti. I have certainly had droughts though my life, too many to speak of really. Now I have my cactus philosophy, grab the sustenance when you can whether it is the rain, a dance in the morning, or feeling the precise movements of a tai chi class. I do not know when I may not be able to do all these things anymore, so I feed my body and soul with them now, for the dry spells. The cacti remind me every day."

I ask, "Are they hard to keep? I mean do you have to be some sort of cactus wrangler to make sure they are healthy?"

Ursula bursts out laughing, "A what? A cactus wrangler! Holy Mary Mother of God I have been called many things but that is most definitely a first! No, they are not hard to keep, but there are different kinds with different needs, sure, just like people!"

I like Ursula. She has a powerful passion for life and all its colours, even neon. I wonder at what the sadness is that she alludes to but dare not ask for fear of changing the mood and maybe spoiling this newly forming connection. I smile at the cactus wrangler comment, I think that is exactly how I will secretly think about Ursula from now on, a collector and wrangler of exotic succulents. She heads up the stairs ahead of me, bedecked in her vivid colours like an exotic bird of paradise, with her bag of sweet treats for the costumed children who will be heading around in a couple of days.

With a wave of her free hand, she ascends to the next floor leaving me to my own door.

I sense eyes on me.

"What does she have on her windowsill?" Sinead asks.

"Cacti! Loads of them," I reply. "I noticed them on the first day I arrived here, just loads and loads of them! I've been meaning to ask her why she has such a fascination with them ever since."

"Hmmm, cacti," Sinead repeats, "I have always thought that they are the perfect plant of solitude, a bit like me really."

"Do you ever go out at all?" I blurt. I had not meant it to be so abrupt a question, an accusation tearing through the air between us like a barbed attack. This is simply not my style, not the way I go on. I think that it is because I get so little "airtime" with Sinead, she normally ducks back in behind her door, her wooden barricade against the rest of the world. I gulp in any more questions.

"Outside does not agree with me." A simple statement, simply put and a lesser person may have left other enquiries hanging in the air and not try to tease out any more information.

"How long is it since you left your place Sinead?" I decide to adopt a slightly more softly, softly approach.

"Oh, let me think ....it must be.... it's got to be.... Two years!" I can see that even stating the amount of time has come as a bit of a shock to her. Two whole years, what must that be like to be indoors for that length of time without venturing outside the door? I find that hard to process. I love my walks to work and the constant changes I discover on my trips to the park. Shades of green, glimpses of the deer as they travel across the park plains to discover the richest shoots. I do not know how I would fare without that opportunity to just be somewhere else, with the opportunity to just pass the time of day. I have often headed down to Park Perks and sat outside to watch the world go by. Four walls sound suffocating.

"That is certainly some length of time," I reply, "how do you manage for shopping and everything?" As I ask, I recall there have been sounds some evenings that must have been store deliveries.

"Online shopping has been the way to go," she says. "I do not have to leave the comfort of my own flat, I can get anything and everything that I need."

"But what about friends?" I ask, feeling rather sad for this woman peering from behind her front door, seemingly consumed by the force sucking her back into the flat. It is as though she has an almost morbid fascination with testing her own resilience and I suspect that this is the longest engagement she has had with a real person during her two-year confinement.

“I keep in touch by email and Skype,” she says, “I much prefer it. Less chance of being...” A sudden stop. No more words. She looks uncomfortable, no more than that, she looks shut down.

I do not know what happened to her two years ago, but I am pretty sure that whatever occurred it had put the almightiest of brakes on her life. I decide then that I should try to help in some way. I do not know quite how I am going to accomplish that, but I will try to find a way; I have discovered I am not too bad at making new starts.

Chapter 8

After my pre-Halloween meetings with both Ursula and Sinead, I decide that maybe I should bring my housemates together, maybe a house meeting of all the flat residents, but is that a bit, oh I don't know, 'twee?' Work is still busy every day and I get to know the residents a bit more with every single shift I work, but I still have not really met properly the other people with whom I share Grove House. I hatch a plan to get my neighbours together.

What might do it? It needs to be more than just a residents' meeting.... something different...something that creates a reason to be together without just relying on chat, a focus!

I look out of the window of my tiny sitting room. Out and down, to the rear of the building where I can just see the residents' car park. There are only three cars parked there including my own rarely used Golf. There is a patch of rough looking briars and weeds under the two trees. It has the air of urban neglect. The gnarly twisting stalks of the briars festooned with menacing thorns. I have always thought that briars have very little to recommend them to the world, not even a flower to bring a petal of joy. Goodness only knows what is lurking beneath them! I always remember that saying; you are never further than 3 metres away from a rat, urghh! The thought of that makes me feel quite queasy. This combination of revulsion and the desire to make something happen, sparks an idea and I resolve to put a plan into action.

I design a notice. I will pop it under all their doors and hang it on the noticeboard just inside the main front door just to be sure. The notice reads as follows:

"Grove House Wilderness Clear Up

Would you like to join me this coming Saturday at 10 am to clear out the briars and weeds next to the car park? Tea, Coffee and Biscuits for workers! Hope to see you then! Angie (Flat 4!)"

I write out the four notes and then walk-through Grove House to deliver to my neighbours. I hope that even one of my housemates decide to come along and I especially hope that Sinead will consider venturing outside. After I deliver the invitations, I make a short list of things that I need, including a few packets of chocolate biscuits. I am rather pleased with myself. Now to do some research on options for getting rid of briars and what to plant in their place. I love a project, and this gardening business is all new to me so I will be learning something as well.

When Saturday arrives, I am up and dressed in my old jeans, jumper and some heavy rubber gloves. I have the biscuits in a bag and a couple of flasks for hot water and a carton of milk. I hope no one takes sugar! I had found some sturdy secateurs and heavy weight garden waste bags in the supermarket, in the centre aisle of course where there is always an array of random household and gardening items. A bread machine had been adjacent to the secateurs, but I had resisted the temptation; unlike several of my fellow shoppers.

I glance at Sinead's door as I head down the stairs. No sign of any movement there, still there is always hope and if I cannot tempt her this time then maybe next time? As I head down the flight of stairs, I hear a faint closing of a door. Ursula or Sinead? My answer comes quickly as sprightly steps come down the stairs. Ursula is sporting a rather fetching, bright green today and the look is completed by red wellingtons and orange gloves. She is a veritable traffic light of colour, and she is ready to bring order to our errant green space.

"Great idea Angie," Ursula beams a radiant smile.

"Just what we all need to bring us together, a project! How wonderful; now then let's get started, sooner we are done the sooner there will be time for a cuppa!" and with that she is off.

Mick's door opens.

"You're in luck," he says, "I'm not in the café today, bit of a loose end truth be told so I'll join your 'wilderness' crew."

"No Leo?" I ask.

"Nah, he'd just be a right pain in the behind if he is not the centre of attention! Maybe when we have got it into some shape I'll bring him down."

A man emerges from the other ground floor flat. He is greying at the temples with salt and pepper hair, I estimate that he is in his late 50s, maybe a little more. His face is oval, a suggestion of laughter lines around his eyes, and he is wearing silver rimmed glasses that he pushes up his nose as he returns my look. I am puzzled, I know this face but how is that possible? I know that I have not seen who lives in that flat and I know that I have not met that many people outside work, could this man be one of the delivery guys who comes to The Beeches? No... I ponder a moment and then realisation hits me, this is the man with the trolley change!

"Two Euro!" I exclaim.

"Jaysis!" he replies. "The trolley lady! You must be Angie, nice to meet you, I'm Tom." He extends his right hand to shake on the introduction.

"Well done on sorting this," Tom says, "nothing like a bit of gardening to bring people together. I used to have an allotment and must confess I really miss it. There was always a lot of camaraderie over growing spuds."

So that is four out of the five. Just one missing and that is Sinead. I wonder if pure curiosity will push her to join us?

Mick and Ursula are already standing to the rear of the building surveying the task ahead of us. Now that I am standing beside the briars, they look enormous and rather menacing with huge thorns, and I am not sure if my new secateurs, sturdy or not, will be able for the task. It turns out that Tom has managed to borrow some long-handled clippers and through this bit of forward thinking, is making this challenge a lot easier. He hacks into the briars, and we cut them up into small pieces to put into the garden waste bags.

There are a lot of ouches and the occasional "feck" followed by laughter. As if by magic, albeit slow and laborious magic, the overgrown area begins to look less threatening, shrinking with every cut and hack. In addition to thousands of weeds we find...A walking boot, three empty vodka bottles, a mangled cot mattress, decaying newspapers, plastic wrappers, and cigarette butts.

The layers of rubbish just kept coming. Some of the paper rubbish is harpooned on the spikes of the briar, forever trapped in thorny clutches. I feel the heat of exertion creep through my body, muscles tingling and my hands feeling the strength of the grip needed to exert pressure on the secateurs.

I am used to being on my feet for long periods with my job and have never shied away from the physicality of work, but this is a different kind of toil, a grimy, muscle-wrenching and exhausting toil. As I look around me, I can see Mick and Tom sweating away as they lop and lift. Ursula is taking the lighter loads and doesn't seem to even glisten with the task.

That'll be the salsa and other exercise classes she takes; I think to myself. The woman is a machine! A mature machine in green! I am a poet.

The work continues for two hours. We are tired, grubby and carrying the war wounds of dealing with the undergrowth.

"Right, I think we all deserve a well-earned break," I say. I take out the flasks, the tea bags and jar of coffee, milk and some mugs I have brought down with me. The biscuits are the last thing to come out.

“Tea or coffee?” I ask each of my co-workers.

Two teas and two coffees later we are sitting on the small red brick wall dunking chocolate digestives into out hot drinks. Despite the coolness of the weather we are all glowing after our exertions. The steam from our hot drinks curls up into the cold autumnal air like thin tendrils of fading gauze and we sip our drinks as we chat.

“You really don’t realise how much space there is under there until all that rubbish is out of the way,” says Ursula

“Bloody hard work,” Tom replies, surveying the scratches and cuts on his arms “But worth it!” he adds rapidly.

“Too right,” says Mick.

“Ah isn’t it great to be out in the air,” Ursula chips in again. I think that she is anxious that I do not feel as though I have burdened them with this labour this morning.

Then something rather strange occurs. The door opens and Sinead is standing there, just inside. I sense that she is hesitating, although I get the impression that she would like to come out to join us.

“Come on out pet!” Tom calls.

“There’s a cuppa and some really nice choccie bikkies,” he tries to entice her.

“I’m grand here for now,” is the reply. I decide to take the mug of tea to Sinead and hand her two biscuits. She accepts them with a flash of gratitude, and I do not pass comment on whether she should venture out of the door to join us. A moment of understanding passes between us. I cannot see the world in the way that she does or imagine what she is thinking when she faces the space beyond the door, but I do know that it has taken some extraordinary strength for her to get this far and that is good enough for me.

“What do you think Sinead?” I ask.

“I have not been out here for a couple of years,” she says. “It looks as though you’ve all done an amazing job getting it cleared so far, what are you planning on doing with it?”

“I am not sure that we have got that far yet!” I laugh. “There’s still a bit of a way to go and I think that we may have run out of steam today, but sure there is always next weekend and I think that we have probably broken the back of it today. Maybe we could all make suggestions as to how we can use the space and perhaps get a kitty together?”

The small group agree to this idea and after some chat, we decide to meet again next Saturday and come up with ideas. I am pleased with myself that we all really pulled together on this and have achieved a lot already. All it takes is a catalyst and things will develop.

Mick comes over to me as the others are packing up.

“I have a mate who works in the building trade, and I think that he may be able to give us some pallets if you think they might be of use when we have this cleared,” he says.

“What would you use pallets for?” I ask, not really understanding how they can be used.

“I’ve seen them being made into all sorts for gardens. Planters, benches, vertical gardens, you name it! They’re only wood after all and free is always a good thing as far as I am concerned. I will do a bit of research and check it out with him.”

Wow, this idea seems to be literally growing.

The following weekend we finish the work of clearing. The resulting space is about a metre wide and about two and a half metres long. There is some dry bare soil and some old paving stones that have not seen the light of day for some considerable time. The removal of the rubbish and the encroaching greenery starts to give an air of possibility and we look at it with optimism.

“Sure, it’ll be a right little sun trap in the summer,” Tom declares.

“Just needs a few bits to take the bareness off, any ideas?”

“I love daffodils and tulips,” says Ursula. “This would be the right time for planting them now, it would make a lovely display in the spring, and we can think about what we could plant then.”

“I was saying to Angie that I may be able to get some bits and pieces off a mate of mine, he works in the building business and might have some handy bits he doesn’t need, always worth a try and save a few bob,” Mick offers.

“Yes, let’s see whether that is a possibility and have a look at prices of packs of bulbs, it would be nice to have colour here early in the year,” I say, and so that is decided.

Mick is despatched to contact his friend and I make plans to drive Ursula out to the nearby garden centre to look at bulbs. This project is making us all come closer together and it feels good.

Ursula and I manage to find a time that works for us to select bulbs. We head to a garden centre on the other side of the Phoenix Park. I have always loved visiting garden centres. A guilty pleasure if you like, with a different atmosphere to any other kind of retail therapy. It is the sensory nature of being in a place laden with the scents and colours of plants, potting compost, wooden trellis and that extra feeling of living things growing around you; the air charged with a primeval energy and growth coming from the basic need to fulfil the promise of some grand plan for each one of these plants. From the moment we enter the garden centre, we are surrounded by a magnificent display filled with waving grasses, their fluffy seed heads bowing to greet us, cheery pink chrysanthemums, and heathers in shades of lilac while flashes of white gather at the base of the grasses like adoring fans clamouring around their favourite celebrity. Ursula and I stop to admire the display and take a note of the plants that have been used, not for today unfortunately, as our budget has been allocated to the things we will need for our spring bulbs.

We walk further into the centre, past shelves of shades and shapes of green foliage. Spikes of flowers reach out and almost touch us as we walk past, silently asking to be taken home and planted so they might grow in new ground and colonise new places. Ursula and I are determined to do what we have come here for and continue until we find what we seek.

“Goodness me!” Ursula exclaims. “Look at the selection they have here! Not your common daffodils for this crowd; how on earth are we going to make a decision with all this choice?”

I see what she sees. Racks and racks of bulbs in all shapes, sizes, and colours. I think that we are going to have to start with trying to get the most we can for the money our neighbours have contributed. I check the kitty.

“We have €100 Ursula, that has to get us a lot of bulbs. Maybe we could look at getting some of the standards that look cheaper and then perhaps put some of the fancier ones in, you know like a focal point; a bit like the grasses at the entrance. What do you think?”

Ursula nods and we start to work our way along the shelves looking for possible purchases. There are a couple of bags of thirty daffodil bulbs that are on offer, and we decide to get them for their buttery yellow flower heads, so that is certainly a good start. Ursula finds a fancy narcissus called “Rip van Winkle” that has petals that look like stars. We decide to get thirty of them as well to mix in with their more modest cousins.

We then alight upon the tulip collection, and they are really 'wow'! Parrot tulips, fringed petal tulips, botanical tulips in candy stripes, lily flowering tulips, double flowered tulips the list goes on. A decision is needed here, someone to take the helm. I nominate Ursula.

"You go ahead Ursula, you pick the colours and the types, I think you have more colour in your life than me, I trust you!"

If you have ever heard that phrase 'like a child in a sweetshop,' that is what sums up Ursula's expression when she is given the green light to go ahead and choose the bulbs. She picks up packets with colourful photographs illustrating the bulbs and carefully considers how the shades would work together. She then looks at flowering times to double check that we will have a nice display for several weeks. After twenty minutes she has her top choices set out and has selected some gorgeous parrot tulips in vibrant scarlet and yellow, some lily tulips in red and white, and lacy petaled magenta ones as a darker contrast. I think that we may have gone a bit mad, but ninety daffodils and fifty tulips later we have our springtime-blooming haul. Ursula disappears for a moment and returns with two of the types of grasses we had seen at the front of the garden,

“Just for a bit of something before all the bulbs come through, my treat,” she winks.

We purchase compost and put everything into my trusty Golf. When we arrive at Grove House, we meet Tom who informs us that he has read in a magazine that it is possible to plant bulbs in big black bins and to layer them up so that they bloom in phases and bring lots of colour. We agree that that sounds like a good idea and Mick contacts his building pal who kindly finds two round bins for us. A couple of days later, he brings them round, tapping his nose and saying that he *found* them; so no charge. We decide not to ask any questions, a nod is as good as a wink, and we set to planting them up, it is like making a “bulb lasagne” with the layers building; ready to be a feast for the eyes when they waken after the winter. Stones in the base of the bins, then sand, then compost and finally the stratification of the bulbs, slightly offset at each layer so they can grow unimpeded. Finally, we plant the grasses at the top in the centre of each bin. The waving stems await their flower accompaniment that will arrive with the warmer weather.

Chapter 9

Why is it that December rolls in so quickly every year? One moment it is the golden hued Autumn, and the next, the nights truly draw in and the shops fill with Christmas decorations and cards (I have seen some shops start doing that in August, but I find Santa and the trappings of the festive season very difficult to process when people are still walking around in T-shirts).

I love the crispness of December mornings and the way my breath is vapour clouds in the air as I walk to work. My bobble hat is pulled down over my ears, my cheeks prickling in the icy air. Cold nose turning red with the chill and being met by the warm air and warm Christmas atmosphere in the reception. The staff room is festooned with Christmas cards on the notice board from families of the residents. There are also an astounding number of goodies that have been dropped in as thank yous for us to have "with a cup of tea," I think we would have to have a hundred tea breaks to even make a dent in the chocolates!

The glimmering decorations and twinkling lights are up in The Beeches and Christmas music plays at work. The crooning 'bubba bubba' of Bing Crosbie singing "Little Drummer Boy," the "Have yourself a merry little Christmas" and "Rocking around the Christmas Tree." This is the soundtrack to my working day. We have set up the Christmas tree in the day room and everywhere is feeling very festive. Our activities calendar is filled with paper chain making, carol singing, mince pie-icing, sugar dusting and a special festive version of bingo with the prizes wrapped in Christmas wrapping paper.

Mick can come in more often in the colder weather. Park Perks has shorter opening hours with the darker evenings as walkers and joggers change their fitness outings to enjoy the reduced daylight. Coffees and teas are enjoyed under patio heaters and the cheery red blankets Mick puts over the seats outside. At this time of year, he closes shop at 3 o'clock and heads down to see Breda most days. She is in better form when he is there, and he has taken to filming videos of Leo on his phone so that she can see what new ridiculous outfit the little monster has been dressed in. I hear her cackling laughter down the corridor when there is a screening of Leo's latest indignity. Tears of laughter accompanied by,

"Awh the poor little blighter, a lilac tutu? Whatever will he think of himself Mick!"

Thursdays are the day our visiting hairdresser comes to the home. Several our ladies like to have a weekly wash and set. Louise has been coming to the home for several years, she charges very little really and the residents love the chats and quite often, the scandals Louise regales them with during their appointments. Louise is so truly kind, and she listens to all the stories and memories each time as if it is the first time she has heard them, and in return the residents get to hear of her rather tumultuous love life. In the words of Breda, Louise has a "heart of gold." A little bit of primping and being made a fuss of is just what the doctor ordered for our residents and the Three Amigos are normally at the front of the queue for their wash and sets, queen bees in a cloud of hairspray. Louise normally comes for a quick coffee in the staff room before she heads off each week and it has been known for her to do a sneaky trim for members of staff on a break. Just another cog in the machine making The Beeches a social place to live rather than a nursing place to exist. We all have our part to play in this like intricate pieces of a social jigsaw puzzle.

As Christmas Day approaches, the Grove House residents decide to organise a Christmas dinner together. None of us have any family nearby. Ursula offers to host us in her top floor flat as she seems to be the only one with a table big enough to sit us all together. We are delighted when Sinead agrees to join us, a tiny communal celebration. We divide the shopping list between us and agree to each have a hand in preparing the vegetables, starters and desserts. I am rostered to work on Christmas Eve and Christmas morning, so I volunteer to make the starter. I keep it simple with smoked salmon and brown bread.

Christmas morning in the Beeches is pure celebration. Our residents are dressed in their festive best and again carols are playing. All the staff are wearing Santa hats. We exchange Kris Kindle gifts in the morning. I receive a beautiful Irish Blessing plaque "Níl aon tinteán mar do thinteán féin" – there's no fireside like your own. I am really touched that one of my colleagues would think to get this for me and feel my eyes becoming a bit watery. I carefully place the gift in my rucksack and at 2 o'clock, head back down the road to Grove House. I must call into the shop to pick up the bottle of prosecco I had promised to bring to the dinner. Kiera was there as usual; I hope that she is getting some amount of overtime for working on Christmas Day. There is a new face beside her, Dominik, standing in front of the till looking perplexed.

"Erm Kiera sorry to bother you again but I cannot see what I put the wrapping paper through on again?" The customer he is serving is not happy at the delay.

Kiera arches her extremely coiffed eyebrows in her co-workers direction and clearly for the hundredth time says, “Granny Smiths!”

I feel some pity for Dominik, it’s not exactly the obvious choice of charging for stationery. Kiera rolls her eyes and tuts in my direction.

“Staff training am I now?” she grins, “Merry Christmas Angie! You been working already today, no rest for us poor workers, wha!”

“Many happy returns Kiera,” I pay for the prosecco and pop the bottle into my rucksack. “Just a half day today, off for my dinner now and I cannot wait!”

“It’s as well for you,” she replies, “I’m on ‘til 6, if I manage to get through it that long.” She looks darkly in the direction of her co-worker and with a theatrical raising of her hand whispers, “This young fella is doing me bleedin’ head in. Earlier on we had one of the regulars in and yer man was on the deli counter. The customer asked for a sausage roll, Dom there asked whether they wanted a big sausage roll or small one. The customer said, “No a sausage roll,” yer man says, “Oh, a large one?” It all kicked off then when the customer shouted, “Are ye feckin stupid, a ROLL with sausages in it...”

Her face becomes serious.

“I suppose this is the sort of thing you get when you are going up the ranks of management,” she pauses, then erupts into laughter. “Have a great afternoon Angie and don’t eat too much turkey!”

A wave and I hear Kiera apologising to the customers who have been delayed by the wrapping paper, Granny Smith apple confusion.

Outside the shop stands Jim examining the greasy contents of a pack of sandwiches. He is wearing a warm coat and has a sleeping bag rolled up and tied with a piece of rope. He speaks, “Any change missus?”

I find I have eight euro in my coat pocket and give it to him. He looks surprised that his request has been acknowledged.

“God Bless, Merry Christmas,” he says and turns to move slowly down the road towards the Park Gate. I feel helpless and a bit guilty walking towards the guarantee of warmth and a meal, it is not a feeling that sits easily with me.

As I go through the front door of Grove House, I can hear “Merry Christmas Everyone” from the very top of the house. There are delicious smells in the hallway. Aromas of cooking turkey, roasting potatoes, buttered cabbage, Christmas pudding. My mouth is watering, but first to clean up, dress up and to get the salmon starter plated and up to Ursula's. My thoughts of Jim and his Christmas Day are still with me, but it is also so exciting to be properly celebrating. I call Paula quickly and wish her a very happy Christmas and thank her for the beautiful hat and scarf she had crocheted for me, so thoughtful and so creative of her. I am really looking forward to her visit next year, she is looking at taking time off at Easter and we are going to do a road trip around Ireland for a few days.

Uniform off, Christmas Day outfit on. Salmon plated and on a tray, to carry up the staircase. One final check in the mirror, a bit of lipstick and that is it - I am not quite Cinderella, and it would be a bit of a stretch to call this a ball – it is only 4 o'clock after all, but it is time to spend with new-found friends and that is what life is about really. I wonder if I should call for Sinead but when I knock there is no reply. Maybe she has changed her mind about going?

I walk up the stairs with my tray of food and a bottle of prosecco tucked under my arm. The door to number 5 is open and the Christmas music is a bit louder. This is the first time I have been into Ursula's flat. It is bedecked with Christmas decorations and a tastefully decorated tree (artificial one she confides in me later). The table is beautifully laid with crystal wine glasses and place setting labels made with mini silver Christmas baubles.

Ursula is in the kitchen, and I can hear her chatting to Mick, the two foodies together talking about flavours, basting and cooking times. The cooking meal wafts out in waves of fragrant aroma. I can feel myself salivating. It was a busy morning and I have not eaten since my breakfast of two pieces of toast at 5.30 am. This dinner is very much anticipated!

Ursula looks up from the stove and flashes her wonderful smile.

"Angie! Ah you're a sight for sore eyes! Delighted you made it!" Her face is the definition of delight and I sense that it is more than my arrival. She is loving having everyone in to share this celebratory meal with her. Mick takes over the stirring of the gravy as she comes over to give me a quick hug. He waves a hello and carries on.

"Now what can I get you?" Ursula asks. "I think that I have most things, just name it," she says.

"Do you know I think that I may just have a soft drink for now," I reply. I am feeling genuinely thirsty and worry that if I have anything stronger then I may just gulp it down and be asleep before the dinner is ready after such an early start.

"How about an elderflower spritzer?" she asks. "I always find them very refreshing, hit the spot just right."

"Sounds delicious, yes please I have not tried that before," I reply and then, "Ursula, where would you like me to put the salmon? Is there room in the fridge?"

"Yes, yes of course, give that to me now and I will put it away, now you go and have a seat you've been working all morning, go on and join Sinead and Tom."

Ursula bustles off carrying the tray and I turn the corner to see Sinead and Tom chatting. Wait, Sinead and Tom chatting.

"Hello, you two Merry Christmas! How are things?" I walk over and give them both a brief hug.

"Grand, we have been having a great chat here. Sinead has been telling me about her job, do you know she can do everything from her own flat on the internet, never needs to head into an office! How about that? Bloody amazing!" Tom is either unaware of Sinead's dislike of leaving the building or is supremely diplomatic.

"There's no great mystique to it really," Sinead replies quietly.

"Enough of that pet, it is pretty amazing from where I am with all this technology!" Tom exclaims.

"I cannot even get the hang of the fancy mobile phones. My daughter keeps telling me to get one, but what would I be doing with it, turning into one of them with their phone in front of their faces all the time. Connected me arse! Cannot imagine a way of being less connected!" He stops abruptly then erupts into laughter.

"Jaysis, listen to me ranting on! Sound like a right ole fogey, pay me no mind I think that I am just a bit scared of all this technology taking over the world and I feel a bit left behind truth be told."

Tom explained he had spent his working life on the buses and had retired in 2017, a fact that he felt quite relieved about now given the ever-extending retirement age. He shares that he had spent his working life behind the wheel, and he now wanted to steer his own course. He does a bit of handyman work locally, just a little to give him a bit of interest.

"Not all technology is bad Tom," says Sinead. "There are all sorts of things you can do just with a smart phone, handy things like your shopping, banking, paying bills, even bus timetables! I can show you if you would like to learn."

I think that this is the longest I have heard Sinead speak. Her face is earnest and open.

Tom takes a moment to think.

"You would do that for me? Now wouldn't that be a surprise for my daughter and her family. They think that

I am still back in the stone age, but it is very difficult to get your head round these things if you are not with the person showing you how to do these things. You are on Sinead! I am going to say a big yes please and thank you to your kind offer!"

Tom offers his hand to shake on the arrangement, Sinead takes it and positively glows as he shakes her hand enthusiastically.

With that Mick walks into the room with a tea towel in his hand and his Park Perks apron on.

"What's all the chat in here then?" he questions, wiping his hands.

"Brokering tuition so we are," replies Tom. "Sinead here is going to turn me into a techie wizard, you will not recognise me."

Sinead smiles, "I am not sure that it is going to be that fundamental of a change Tom, but we will give it a go, you could be the social media king of the North Circular Road!"

"Like that Whatterberg fella?" exclaims Tom. "Now that would be a sight to see!"

The conversation carries on with the chat turning to favourite Christmas memories, corny jokes. Then the main event: the meal itself.

Ursula has worked wonders with the starter. She has decorated the plates with capers, jewel red cherry tomatoes and delicate feathery sprigs of dill. It all looks just so pretty. We all take our places at the table. Ursula at the head as our host. We toast each other with a glass of the prosecco I had brought and settle down to a truly splendid Christmas dinner. After the first course, we take a short comfort break before the main event.

The beautifully bronzed turkey has been resting to make sure that it is just right. The crispy skin looking like burnished amber twinkling in the fairy lights. Mick brings the bird to the table and in turn, each of us go into the kitchen to bring out one of the serving dishes. Buttered carrots, brussels sprouts with crispy pancetta chopped through them, golden roast potatoes and parsnips, chestnut stuffing and cocktail sausages. The table is heaving under the weight of all the food. Mick carves and serves the aromatic slices, an ambrosial sensory journey back to Christmas past. We sit suspended in expectation of the meal to come. When everything is brought out, we are under starter's orders.

"A Toast!" Tom exclaims. We raise our glasses.

"Here's to the chefs! May the hinges of our friendship never grow rusty!"

Glasses are clinked and the consumption begins.

The room is quiet, bar the sound of enjoying good food. Mumbles of “This is good” and “Have you tried?” then more nondescript murmurs of a good meal enjoyed. Small talk, sips of wine, replete with this beautiful meal. A pause.

“Can anyone manage Christmas Pudding yet?” Ursula almost teases us with that question.

“Not yet I could not manage another bite,” I reply. “Could we have a little break?”

I think again about Jim and his measly sandwich, once again feeling quite guilty at the feast I have consumed.

“I think it may need to be a bit more than a little break!” Tom chips in. “How about a game?”

Ursula points over to some games set out on the table and one that catches my eye. I had always loved playing this board game with Paula and the girls, especially if we played after an evening out! I leave the still-laden dinner table and head over to the box.

“This one,” I say, “let’s play this.”

“Good choice,” says Mick. Space is made on the table and the box is unpacked. Cards, board, counters and the tiny sand timer are placed on the table.

“Now how are we going to do this?” Ursula asks. “We are an odd number so how will we organise the teams?”

Sinead speaks, “I don’t mind watching, you all go ahead and play.” As she spoke it was as though she faded slightly in her place at the table, expecting to be allowed to back away from the group and into her own thoughts and space.

“Not at all!” we all exclaim, and resolve to rotate the clues and guessing. I am not sure that we play it in the way that the manufacturer intended, but there is laughter aplenty and soon the counters on the board are forgotten as we all start guessing together. It is raucous and loads of fun and in the midst of us Sinead is most definitely present in the room.

The pudding is presented to appreciative applause after we have concluded our game. Ursula pours brandy over the top and lights it. The dome of the rich pudding dances with a blue flame, skittering over the surface and dying moments later. We all have a piece and pour cream over the top.

“Heart attack special on a plate,” Tom winks, and tucks into his first spoonful.

Once again, the sounds of convivial eating rise from us. A few more glasses of wine followed by teas and coffees. I look at the clock on the mantlepiece and cannot believe it is nearly 10 o’clock. Dusk, then darkness has crept around Grove House without us noticing. The brightness in our spirits and the fairy lights bedecking the tree have distracted us from the short day. Crispness has crept slowly behind the loss of the day to bring an icy glisten to the trees outside.

"Do any of you know that man Jim, the homeless guy who is often round here?" I ask.

Mick responds, "Yep I think everyone knows Jim around here, lovely fella, has too much of a fondness for the gargle though and it has landed him in awful situations."

"I saw him earlier, at least he is wearing a thick coat now, but all the same...."

"I gave him my dad's old coat," Mick says, "Jim often calls by the café, and I normally give him a cuppa and a bite to eat, couldn't see him go without, he used to do a few bits for my mam when he was younger."

The conversation continues for a while, and I piece together Jim's story. He has always lived locally, but the loss of a child and the subsequent breakdown of his marriage had led to another relationship in his life, alcohol. The others said that he normally stayed in a hostel down towards the Liffey but headed back in this direction daily because he felt safer here in his old neighbourhood. It was good to hear that Mick helped him out with a bite to eat and clearly in other ways, but what an existence. Guilt engulfed me again. I have had to deal with difficulties, but I realise it is a fine line whether we conquer challenges or succumb to them.

Our festive evening is coming to an end, we clear up all the plates and pans working in our own pleasant chain gang of washing up, drying and stacking. It takes no time at all.

“I know we said that we would not do gifts,” Ursula says coyly, “but I wanted to give each of you something, just a token of how much I have appreciated today and the opportunity to share it with you.”

“Now then Ursula there was no need for that, you’ll be making a show of us all,” Tom gently chastises her, but with a smile in his eyes.

“You may not be thanking me for the gifts,” she replies and turns to the windowsill.

“At some stage you have all been curious about my cacti,” she begins, “I have decided to give one as a gift to each of you, so you see it really is not such a big thing.”

It is only now that I notice there are four of the cacti in brightly coloured pots with ribbons tied around them and a label on each.

Ursula examines the first cactus.

“This is yours Tom, a barrel cactus also known as the mother-in-law cushion. It’s not going to be too much work as it only needs to be watered every two to three months." She hands the cactus to a bemused Tom who thanks her and examines his gift.

"Barrel cactus Ursula? Are you suggesting that I may be getting a bit plump in my retirement?" Tom quips, but we can see that he is rather touched by the gift.

"For you Sinead I have chosen this star cactus. It doesn't get very big and has lovely yellow and white flowers. I hope you like it."

Sinead looks genuinely delighted by this gesture and accepts her gift with a quiet, "Thank you".

"Now you Angie, I had to think about the one to give you and I made a decision that I hope you will like. This is a moon cactus. It is a hybrid of two cacti and that seems to be quite appropriate with your Irish and English heritage. They do need a bit of looking after, but you are in the caring profession, so I hope you are up to the task!"

I think 'no pressure then,' as I accept this quirky and strangely apt present.

"Finally, Mick this is the bunny ears cactus, yes you heard me right! It does not have spines but is covered in polka dots. You are the true animal lover amongst us here! I thought it might be safer if Leo is around, the last thing we would want would be for him to be prickled!"

This was quite an honour. Ursula loved each one of her cacti and to be given one felt very special.

I feel as though I have joined a rather special club 'The Cactus Growers Club'.

Then Ursula exclaims, "Oh, I nearly forgot! The most important part is that you give your cacti names, every single one of mine has a name, makes it easier when you are chatting to them! Not just a hey you!" She looks expectantly at each of us.

Tom goes first, "I am calling mine Beryl! Its nearly barrel and I can imagine that suiting a mother-in-law rather well!" We all laugh.

"What about you Sinead? What will you call yours?" Ursula enquires.

"Hmmm let me think, a star cactus you say? I think I'll call it Stella and I guess I should refer to it as her from now!"

Another great name that we applaud.

"And our lovely Angie next, what will your cactus be called?" Ursula is determined to keep the pressure on.

"Well like Sinead I am going to be guided by the type of cactus and I am going to call mine Luna. That means that we will have two celestial cacti in the house, not bad for the North Circular Road!"

"Stella, Luna, Beryl they are all ladies. Mick will you keep this trend going or will your cactus be a fella?"

Mick is clearly thinking about this. His brow is furrowed, this type of naming is serious business and should not be hurried, clearly Ursula had not read that memo!

"I am going to call mine Bugs, like Bugs Bunny Ears. I guess that makes it a boy! It will be me, Leo and Bugs, all lads together."

Clutching our new plant friends, we hug and bid our goodnights and leave with our gifts and a sense that this has been an infinitely better day than it would have been alone.

Chapter 10

The conviviality of Christmas continues through the following days. I have a few shifts to do at work, but the days are pleasant with family and friends visiting. Mick is in with Breda every day and even manages to smuggle Leo into her room disguised as a gift-wrapped box.

I am carefully following the care instructions Ursula has given me and Luna is thriving on my windowsill in the dull December daylight. I realise that I am having a chat with Luna every day, telling her about what has happened at work and what is occurring outside the window. It is strangely therapeutic, and the beauty of these one-sided conversations is that she does not answer back or disclose the things I would rather not have spoken of.

New Year's Eve is another spent with my fellow Grove House residents. Our game of choice this evening is charades and the enthusiasm for the play is positively contagious. The clues and guesses become more outrageous as we head towards 2020 and just before midnight strikes, our glasses are filled and we toast to the promise and hope of the New Year before we sing Auld Lang Syne. We are delighted that we have found our tribe and I am so very lucky that this is where I have landed, I think that Dad and Auntie have been looking after me like guardian angels.

January 1st marks the beginning of my first full calendar year living in Ireland. Even the rawness of the morning cannot detract from my sense of well-being and high spirits about this new year and new personal milestone.

In The Beeches we start to take down a number of the Christmas decorations to be stored away. This is a process that takes a few days because the tree is left fully decorated until the 6th January, Women's Little Christmas[3], marking the end of the festive period. It is only then that the baubles are individually enveloped in tissue paper and layered into storage boxes that will be put away in the attic space. The tree is disassembled, and filaments of fake fir drop to the floor like a real tree dropping its needles at the end of the Christmas season. Lights are rolled on to cardboard reels ready for illumination at the end of the year; I always think that rooms seem naked and a little bit sad after the lights and

3 The Feast of the Epiphany is also celebrated as Nollaig na mBan or Women's Little Christmas on 6th January every year.

tinsel have been stored in boxes. Maybe that is what makes January the darkest month, with everyone having Christmas bills to pay and no more glitz and glitter to liven our living spaces.

Maureen is getting the diary of activities together and everyone is looking forward to new programme of events. We have secured a physiotherapist who does a programme of seniors chair-based exercises to promote flexibility and balance. The Three Amigos have christened such activities chairobics and are keen to be involved. More arts and crafts are on the cards as well and we have a musician coming in for a weekly singalong. I am really looking forward to music filling

The Beeches, the lilt of tunes along the corridors has a hugely positive effect on residents and staff alike. 2020 is shaping up to be looking very good indeed.

My morning walks to work are uneventful and my steps meet the pavement with a slight crunch of the frost underfoot. The trees that line my route are suspended in their winter dormant state; saving their energy to endure the coldest season when sunlight is fleeting. It is now a fortnight into 2020 and my strolling commute is accompanied by the radio. The big news this morning is a mysterious new type of pneumonia in an area of China called Wuhan. My geography is not great, and I have no idea where Wuhan is other than what the radio report says, that it is a region in China and apparently an industrial heartland there. The illness sounds serious, as the reporter is saying that the authorities there have put the City and surrounding areas into lockdown and that residents must stay in their homes. It all sounds pretty drastic, but we have heard these things before with bird flu and swine flu and it is on the other side of the world, not much chance of the virus making its way to my leafy Dublin Street.

When I arrive at The Beeches there is chat about the situation in China. A couple of the girls come from the Philippines and their families have said that they have also heard about the new “flu”. As we go about our jobs during the day, we share our thoughts on what might be the extreme response to what the news pundits are calling a novel virus. It is hard to imagine a flu is garnering so much attention in the international media.

I arrive home and switch on the television news to see the report from Wuhan about a flu type virus that seems to have originated in one of the wet markets there. The news report shows that the streets in Wuhan are deserted and there are a few ex-pats who are being interviewed and begging to be allowed to return home, some in dire need of medication which is running out. The footage shows drones relaying orders that citizens are to remain inside their homes. This illness is not like some of the flus we have seen coverage of previously. A different animal altogether and one which is rather unnerving.

I have my dinner and then Facetime Paula. She is cosied up on her sofa and has a steaming cup of tea in her hands, all ready for a chat.

"Hi P, how are things?" I ask.

"Great Ange, its fab to see you, you are looking well. Tell me how was Christmas and New Year? I was thinking of you working over the break how was that?"

"Would you believe it, it was great P. Had a fantastic Christmas dinner with the other people who live here, it was so good we decided to do it again for New Years!"

"So, what are they all like?" Paula asks, I have not really said much about The Cactus Growers' Club other than list the names and their flat numbers. This is the first chance I have had.

"Well, they are a mix of ages, all very different actually," I go on to describe Ursula, Sinead, Tom and Mick in turn and finally tell Paula about our induction into Cactus ownership. I am not sure that she is convinced of the wisdom of the decision. I have not had a lot of luck with houseplants in the past. Paula had once asked me to look after her Areca Palm and I managed to kill it off after ten days; she had not been happy. Paula tells me about her job and her utter lack of love life then we get to discussing her visit.

“I am just so excited Angie,” she says. “I am so looking forward to seeing the places you have talked about and taking a walk through that wonderful park. We will have to keep our fingers crossed that the weather will be good to us and that we will be able to get out and about without getting soaked.” Paula does not get many days holiday entitlement a year and this trip is a big deal, I plan to make it very special for her.

We briefly mention the events in China; a “Did you hear?” and a “Yes I did, those poor people trapped in their homes, that’s what you get for a government who can impose without challenge.”

That was the end of the chat and now my bed is calling me. On the other side of the world there is an unsettling spread of the virus continuing.

As January progresses, the other big news here is the forthcoming general election campaign trail. I watch with interest, the party promises relating to housing and health spends including promises of funding for home carers. I always think that if the money that every contending politician claims they will put into action relating to education, health and housing was made available then there would be nothing for their successors to do! It will not be long before the electoral signs are hung along the trees and lampposts on all the main thoroughfares through the city. The Taoiseach will be defending his premiership and the political pundits say that the battle between the two parties will be 'closely fought.'

Since the wonderful Christmas get togethers, I make a point of calling on each of my neighbours at least once a week. We compare notes on how our cacti are faring and it is a reason for the tap on the door and a 'how are things going' conversation. The visits and chats dissipate the grey clouds of January are as much a distraction as anything else. I cannot wait for the brighter days to return.

Ursula's Tai Chi has moved indoors for the colder months, and she has joined a seniors' choir in the local parish centre. Her early morning salsa dancing is now interspersed with the alto parts of whatever piece they are practising in a particular week. She jokes that altos never get to sing the actual melody of a song and I am not sure that she is entirely happy with that situation.

Tom has been kept busy with some painting and clearing work just down the road. He proudly declares to me each visit that 'Beryl' has not yet 'gone to meet her maker.' I get the impression that Tom is rather fond of his botanic mother-in-law. I regularly spot him out at the back of Grove House weeding and tidying our reclaimed garden space.

When I have a day off, I sometimes go for a walk with Mick, who is on reduced winter hours now. We take Leo out for a stroll. The little dog receives many admiring looks for his winter wear. Mick is good company, and the conversation flows easily. He has lots of interests and eagerly shares stories of the park and living in Dublin as he was growing up. He tells me about the historic buildings and even offers to take me on a real 'Dub's' tour of the city. He is worried about his mum, and I reluctantly share with him that I have noticed that Breda is slowing up a little from her usual feisty self.

Finally, Sinead. Our chats take place 'on my own doorstep.' I sense that Christmas has made a big difference and understand that the technology tutoring has started. Apparently, Tom is a good student!

Work rolls forward like the flow of the Liffey. My early starts give me a different perspective on the place where I live. The trees that line my morning route to work are dark and skeletal with leafless fingers reaching into the January air. The news playing in my ears. Traffic updates. Politicians' statements. Brexit. Then a thunderbolt.

“The World Health Organization (WHO) declared a Public Health Emergency of International Concern.”

What is this? Surely this is something isolated to an area of China, Wuhan? How is something so far away becoming a public health emergency? It looked as though everything was being very intensively managed in China.

When I arrive at work there is an air of sadness. One of our residents passed away in the night. Catherine, or Kate as she preferred to be called, was one of our line dancing, bingo playing residents. She brought fun to all the activities and her family were constantly in and out to her, all showing the same zest for life. It was a peaceful passing in her sleep. The doctor had been called and her family had been notified. We all had the opportunity to say farewell to her.

Something that I think is wonderful about Ireland is the way that a life is celebrated. In England, a funeral can take weeks to transpire, but here it is three days. Arrangements are made and families can say goodbye to their loved ones. I remember when my aunt passed away, I felt as though I was in limbo for weeks. Maureen supports Kate’s daughters and son in making the arrangements with the funeral directors. The process is caring and dignified. I attend the removal with some of my colleagues the night before the funeral. There are tears and hugs and a crowd with fond memories of this lovely woman. Maureen and Niamh attend the funeral the following day and they tell us that it was a beautiful service. Kate had been involved in many things before she arrived with us at the Beeches and her surviving family were supported in turn by their friends. A community wrapping their care and support around the family.

Chapter 11

"A Chinese tourist has died in France after contracting the new coronavirus - the first fatality from the disease outside Asia.

The victim was an 80-year-old man from China's Hubei province."

I am getting used to hearing the updates now, on what they are calling the novel coronavirus. People on the news who are living in China and asking for repatriation to their own countries. Planes being despatched to take nationals home and that unsettling set of reports that have started mentioning cases in other places and more worryingly in Europe, but that still seems far away and after all, Ireland is an island sitting on the edge of Europe. My sense of unease is not allayed by Alicia and Camilla, the two girls from the Philippines who are talking about the virus in the staff room. Alicia has a family friend who is critically ill in hospital with the virus, and it is not looking good for them.

We have a new resident, Bill, at The Beeches. He is in Kate's old room. Bill is a local and has moved in after a series of falls. His daughters have persuaded him that this might be the best solution and Maureen was delighted to hear that The Beeches was recommended to Bill's family by several people. It is always good to know that you are doing a decent job and that residents and their families are happy with the care you provide. Bill had worked as an accountant in his earlier years and is a natural comedian who finds the humour in every situation. He always has a quip or a joke for staff and residents alike and proves universally popular. His mind is sharp and his wit sharper. His daughters and grandchildren adore him, and it is delightful to see them together. He asks me or one of the other girls to get bags of sweets for him and has a particular penchant for anything that is as far from denture friendly as we can find. He jokingly calls the sweets 'contraband.' I always nod and wink conspiratorially, and then bring something sugary in the following day. He is a delight. The Three Amigos have taken a particular liking to him and he to them. I often see the four of them gathered with much raucous guffawing. I think that Bill's presence has taken years off the ladies and added applications of lipstick at the same time.

Bill's arrival also rejuvenates the activities in the day room. He is an enthusiastic player of bingo and a bit of a shark at draughts. If anyone was going to fill the space Kate had left in the social side of The Beeches, I think that we would have been hard put to find a better candidate. He manages to bring a smile to the faces of staff and residents alike. Even Niamh blushes when he calls her "Beautiful," and she is a certainly a tough nut to crack.

On the way home I hear, "The first report of the new coronavirus - or COVID 19 – has occurred on Irish shores. It is a woman who travelled through Dublin Airport on her way home to Northern Ireland from a holiday in northern Italy. She has tested positive for the illness on returning home to Belfast."

Without invitation this novel coronavirus has managed to cross the world and walk into the country. Maybe we will be lucky? Perhaps this will be the only case, maybe it is nothing to worry about?

The advancement of the virus is like an itch that is refusing the be scratched. The encroachment across Europe is not stopping. Every day now there are more reports of cases, and the government responses are sounding more serious.

The news reports, "A secondary school in the east of the country closed for 14 days after it was confirmed that a male student has the virus. He had returned from northern Italy, after being in an at-risk area."

There is much conjecture about where the case is, and an unnerving sense that somehow flood gates are about to open. International news reports are showing deaths among vulnerable older citizens and Northern Italy is particularly hard hit. It is heart breaking to see the news footage of intensive care units in Italian hospitals and the coffins literally piling up in churches. How are these events real? The scenes are almost apocalyptic in nature and the shots of empty streets are frightening. Talk of society shutting down to prevent the spread of this virus is no longer the realm of faraway places but is knocking at our door.

I meet Ursula on the landing.

"So, what do you think to all this coronavirus business?" she asks.

"It's all a bit of a worry really Ursula," I reply, "it seems as though it is hitting the older population much harder and to be honest with you, I find it very upsetting to see all the news reports from Italy. Hard to know what to think really, I wonder how we will manage it if it spreads here...."

"I think it will be time to pull up the drawbridge a wee bit," Ursula says with a note of defiance in her voice.

This is a woman with a huge zest for life and I think that it may well take more than a westward bound virus to knock her back.

We go our separate ways. I am genuinely troubled by everything that I am hearing from the health experts and how quickly this virus spreads. Working in a residential home makes me even more cognisant of the issues with the elderly and how vulnerable they are. I have another creeping fear, which is how this will be physically managed in the home. In a hospital everyone is well versed in infection control, but this is not the case at The Beeches, it has never been an environment where it is necessary to think about managing contagion, I worry about this.

My concerns are beginning to take form when I get into work the following day. Maureen and Niamh call a staff meeting. It is not good news.

"Good morning, everyone," Maureen opens the meeting. "I am sure that you are wondering why we have called you all together this morning. In the light of this coronavirus spread we have been issued with a briefing from HIQA[4]. They have said that to reduce the possibility of the spread of the virus they are going to suspend their routine inspections of all residential homes. We have been informed that inspections will be replaced by fortnightly telephone calls and as part of those telephone updates we will be required to make returns relating to staff and residents."

We all sit in silence. It is not the fact that there will not be inspections that is the cause of concern, but this is BIG. Such measures would not be implemented lightly.

Niamh takes over from Maureen, "We have all seen on the news reports that this virus is highly infectious, and it seems that it is possible for people to carry it without displaying symptoms. Our biggest concern obviously, is that mortality is very high amongst the older population. Nursing homes Ireland have decided to restrict visitors to homes with immediate effect and this is a protocol we are going to follow here to help protect all of us. Does anyone have any questions?"

There are a few questions asked:

4HIQA – Health Information & Quality Authority. HIQA's Older People's inspection team are legally responsible for the monitoring, inspection and registration of designated centres for older people, such as nursing homes, in Ireland.

“How are we going to manage if someone here does contract the virus?”

“Will we have protective clothing available to us? What about masks? We are hearing that all this is necessary in hospitals to deal with patients with the virus – what about us?”

“What will happen to the residents? How will we explain all this to them?”

They attempt to provide answers and are understanding, but to be fair, I do not think that Maureen or Niamh are able to answer any of the questions fully. They are as much in the dark as we are about how this will really affect us. It feels like a bomb is ticking and there is no hope of diffusing it before devastation hits.

It is hard to do a day’s work after hearing this news, but it becomes clear that the interaction with the staff is even more important to the residents now that we are not allowing visitors into The Beeches. That means all the visitors; including activities co-ordinators, hairdressers, podiatrists, bingo callers as well as all the family members who call in to see their loved ones. We are their only break from life in the home and that has its own pressures. The chatter and excitement of the weekly activities is gone.

This is all extremely hard to take in, I still feel like the new girl sometimes and now this. I can sense the anxiety gathering like a sea swell, prompting a faint sense of nausea and, not to put too fine a point on it, fear. When I moved here it had been to have a new life that had new opportunities and a chance to redefine myself. I had not even vaguely anticipated something so left field and now it is a reality, I am at a loss as to how I need to deal with it.

The news bulletins are coming thick and fast, and I am consuming every single morsel of them as fast as I can. The nightly announcements are coming from the Department of Health on Baggot Street. The huge brown glassy edifice juxtaposed by the modern sculptures in front of the main doors.

Then.

We lock down.

Thursday the 12th of March 2020. This is the day of the announcement telling the country that we will be locking down. What does that mean?

The Taoiseach addresses the nation. He says that the Government have been mobilising during the past week. From 6 o'clock the measures are put in place, and we are told that they will stay in place until the 29th of March.

I listen in shock, that swell of worry continues to grow. Schools, colleges, and childcare facilities will close. No mass gatherings over one hundred people indoors or five hundred outdoors. We are told to go to our places of work if necessary, but if we can work from home then we should do so. That is obviously the go to work option for me then, unless I bring some of the residents home! We are advised to reduce our social interactions as much as possible and try to stagger break times and working times. The Taoiseach speaks of healthcare workers being on the front line and how we must take responsibility to help them so that they can help those who are most in need. He says finally that we all need to look out for each other. Never a truer word spoken.

The address continues; shops can remain open and the government are trying to ensure that supply chains continue to work. I am pleased to hear that the restaurants and cafes may stay open, but they are required to find ways of implementing public health advice on social distancing. I am relieved for Mick, at least his business will be able to continue to operate and he can make his living.

A new set of reports on the television and radio. Queues of people hoarding toilet rolls and the supermarket shelves being emptied with arguments breaking out in the supermarket aisles. This evidence does not seem to be in the spirit of looking out for each other.

I find a note under my front door.

"The Cactus Growers Club – house meeting in our garden. 2 o'clock Saturday."

On the calendar this is the St Patrick's weekend, my first one in Ireland and one that I had really been looking forward to. Alas no parade, but at least there is now the prospect of socialising outside work.

Saturday morning arrives with a glint of sunshine and the promise of warmer weather. I spend the morning cleaning and tidying and looking forward to the house get together later today.

First thing is first. I have not had the opportunity to talk to Paula since all these announcements have been made. The Facetime button is pressed, and a steaming cup of coffee is at the ready, ascending spirals of visible heat wisping from the revitalising liquid. The wait tone rings. There she is my dear friend, also clutching a mug of coffee.

"Good morning my lovely!" Paula greets me and waves a slice of buttered toast at the camera.

"Good morning to you too!" I return the wave, but my response is with my cereal spoon. We are just so rock and roll!

It could not be said that Paula and I have ever had a problem with awkward pauses and the chat flows about work and life and then of course about the pandemic. I tell her about the situation here and the lockdown restrictions that are in place.

Paula looks shocked.

"Lockdown?" she exclaims, "What everything closed down? That is not what we are being told, are you sure that's not an overreaction? We are not being told anything like that here." She pauses and reflects for a moment.

"I have to say that I was pretty shocked myself Paula. My work has already locked down, no visitors. They are really worried about the residents and how this virus is killing off so many elderly people. I am finding it difficult, so goodness knows what the impact is really going to be on the residents, particularly those who have dementia, they do not understand what is going on and why the normal day has changed so much."

"A lockdown though Angie! Surely that is something that is being put in place where there are lots of deaths, it is not that bad in Ireland is it? I mean why are we not hearing that we should restrict what we are doing here? I am totally confused!"

I see the flash of disbelief on Paula's face. I know what I say next is going to be important.

"Paula, this is serious. I do not know how all this is going to work out, but whatever else is going on please be careful. Our Taoiseach is a medical doctor, and he is definitively saying that we need to stay at home if we can and to stop this spreading. The problem is the expectation of the health system being overwhelmed. We have all seen the news reports from Italy and the way the hospitals are simply overflowing..."

We continue chatting. The talk turns to her planned visit at Easter. Paula remains excited, but I have a strong suspicion that we may have to rethink our plans. Our government instructions are that we need to follow restrictions to "flatten the curve" but will that be reality? We sign off our Facetime call and agree to chat the following weekend. Time has flown while I have been chatting to Paula. It is disquieting that the messages in England are so different, and it makes me think that inconsistency of approaches across countries is the thing that makes it easy for the virus to cross borders. I feel grateful that at least there seems to be some movement here to stop the virus spreading, but can this be enough in isolation?

I decide to get all my chores out of the way before I meet the others in the garden. A fun filled morning of laundry, polishing, vacuuming, bathroom cleaning. I am like a marigold wearing whirlwind bearing cleaning sponges and polish. Is there anything more gratifying than the feel of a completely clean space? I hang my clean clothes on my clothes horse and that is it all done!

I have a shower, cleaning the shower as I do. Thank goodness no one can see me as I scrub the glass screen. I get myself ready and grab some biscuits to take down to the garden with me. I meet Ursula on the landing. She is well insulated in a green jumper with a fluffy orange scarf around her neck.

"You are looking the part for the St Patrick's Day weekend Ursula" I remark with a grin.

"Green is one of my favourite colours, my poor departed husband, God Rest His Soul, always said that green was made for me to wear, that it brought out my eyes." She did a twirl and then waved the ends of her scarf at me.

"Layered it up though Angie, you know what they say, 'don't cast a clout 'til May is out'." Ursula gives a naughty wink as she lifts her jumper a little to reveal a thermal vest.

"Ooh you little rascal Ursula," I laugh, "you'll be giving the lads the wrong idea!"

This makes her explode with laughter.

"Chance would be a fine thing, Angie! Come on let us go down and shock the others!"

We arrive at our reclaimed garden area. Mick is already there with Leo dressed as a leprechaun. His outfit is fitted over his head and his front legs are poked into the legs of the leprechaun with imitation arms holding a pot of gold. The whole look is comic in the extreme. Mick's large tricolour badge reading "The Luck of the Irish" seems very tame by comparison. I feel distinctly underdressed in this company. Sinead comes as far as the door and props it open waving at us. Tom emerges with a flask and cups in his hand.

"Good afternoon to you all, my cactus growing friends!" he calls to us. He hands a cup to Sinead and pours steaming milky coffee into it. He then heads over to the rest of us.

"Well! Look at all the green! Good to see you all. Delighted that we can get together like this. I thought Saturday may be better to get together to mark St Patrick's Day, I know that it is a bank holiday, but I recall that Angie is working on the actual day?"

I am impressed by his recall. It was three weeks ago I mentioned the roster to him and said I was disappointed that I would not be able to go to the St Patrick's Day parade. Now no one is going to the parade, or any parade, as they are not permitted this year. Now I am at a gathering of my housemates, and I am going to enjoy every moment.

"Are you all right over there Sinead? Do you want to come over a little more?" Tom calls, but Sinead waves her mug and gives a thumbs up.

"Right then folks this is not only a meet up, it is lovely to see you all. This is also to chat about all these restrictions and to check in with everyone to see how everyone is getting on and if anyone needs anything?"

Heads nod. We all appreciate that we have established a connection and Grove House community.

Tom continues, "We have all been hearing about this COVID thing and now we are facing a lockdown it is time that we think of ways we can help each other. We cannot know how this is going to go."

Despite the sunshine, the mood becomes sombre.

I speak, "That is a great idea, Tom. At work we have already seen the home closing off from visitors and all the normal ways of life there. I think that despite what we are hearing on the news reports, this is going to get much worse. I fear how this is going to pan out and until now I was feeling quite alone with my fear." I pause and can feel prickles of tears starting to rise.

Ursula comes to me and pats my arm. Her face is a picture of compassion and worry.

"We know Angie, this is frightening. It is only natural to be scared but remember that we have each other here and we will do what we can." Ursula looks at me earnestly and meets my gaze with her own.

Quiet.

"So, what are you thinking Tom," Mick asks.

"I am sure you are watching the news. Even going to the supermarket seems to be like running the gauntlet. My thinking is that if one of us with a car is heading out then maybe we can make a point of checking in with the rest to see is they need anything. It is just being conscious of others really and we will make this all work fine."

"Definitely sounds like a plan to me," Mick says. Leo is sniffing around under the trees and then decides to lay down presenting a peculiar picture as the leprechaun legs must fold in front of him.

I see Sinead wave.

"I have another idea everyone," she says, "I have done my shopping online for the past two years, maybe we could look at something like that?"

“Another clever idea Sinead!” Tom replies. He turns to the rest of us and tells us that Sinead has been coaching him in the use of his recently purchased smart phone. He says it is a revelation and is delighted with the fact that he can chat with his relatives ‘face to face.’ This is a vastly different Tom from the man at Christmas confessing to being a technophobe.

“Sinead has the patience of a saint!” Tom declares.

“Tom you are a fantastic student, no patience was required,” Sinead looks happy. Tom’s acknowledgement of her idea and her help visibly, increasing her confidence.

I am not the only one who is utterly unsettled by this pandemic. The Cactus Growers’ Club is banding together, and I am reassured that being in a different country does not mean that I am isolated.

Chapter 12

It seems like a blink since the Government announcement was televised, encouraging us to “flatten the curve” and to help protect the health system. However, it is an impactful blink and is reflected in every moment at home and work. The streets are quiet, like an old-fashioned Sunday afternoon when I was growing up and everyone said they were ‘bored.’ The only difference now is that we all have a plethora of distractions with the internet, Netflix, and countless ways of connecting with the world. Unfortunately, this means that we are overloading on news of the pandemic along with fake news of what is going on.

There are mixed views of the Government lockdown response here in Ireland as I hear people comparing here to the UK and even the US. It seems to me that actions to keep the vulnerable as safe as they can be can only be right. The other side of that is the sadness I can see in both Mick and his mum Breda through the enforced separation. This sense of loss and sadness permeates the residents in the home, but also the staff who are physically distant from their families with no immediate prospect of seeing them again. The sense of responsibility and pressure is growing.

We now have weekly briefings in work specifically relating to COVID, well, weekly if there have not been intervening HIQA updates or report requirements. We gather in the staff room each time with a mounting sense of trepidation, but also just a sense of being overwhelmed, these instructions are all very well, but we are operating on restricted resources and not all of us are trained nurses and this is very much a nursing situation.

Maureen starts, "Welcome everyone I just want to update you on the current position. We are trying to source PPE[5] for you all. This is proving quite challenging as the world and his wife are trying to do the same thing. There will be shipments of PPE arriving in Ireland, but it is all earmarked for hospitals and it looks as though we are going to have to be resourceful and try alternative routes, as well as approaching the Department of Health. I have got some masks and gowns but, given the levels of requirements from HIQA, I already know that they will not be enough."

5 Personal Protective Equipment

The irony of our situation does not escape those in the room. We are one of those frontline groups we keep hearing about on the news and we are dealing with the most vulnerable group succumbing to COVID but because we work in a private care home environment, we do not have the access to the protective equipment that is being sourced centrally.

I feel as though everything is closing in on me again. This faceless threat is out there lurking, and we do not know its next move other than it is highly infectious and transmissible. If this was a Hollywood movie there would be a plot to follow, and I could be the hero of my own storyline. I imagine myself "tooled up" to defend against the impending villain of the pandemic; that is a laugh, we cannot even get hold of simple face masks and aprons, let alone 'tools!' If only COVID could be quashed as easily as monsters or zombies.

I ponder this idea of being the hero though, and what I can do to take the initiative. The conversation with my Grove House friends about how we can pull together to support each other keeps running through my head and I wonder if there is anything else that I can do. There must be something I can do.

The meeting continues and we discuss all the new protocols and how we are going to manage if we do get a case of COVID here. The resident will have to be kept separate from everyone else and there will have to be infection controls in place that most of the staff are simply not experienced in. That is not the least of our problems, the home is not laid out in segregated sections to combat contagion. The Beeches is an old house that has been repurposed as a care home and the layout presents difficulties when it comes to keeping people effectively isolated. Then of course, there is how the limited number of staff will manage working with a resident with COVID, then having to work with other residents who are not infected. What could possibly go wrong? The meeting concludes with promises of acquiring more PPE and supporting us in our work.

The residents are becoming increasingly stressed by the lack of visits and the lack of activities in the home. This is taking its toll on everyone. I rack my brain as to what might help?

I know that I cannot deal with the massive things, but that I can try to come up with small things that might make a difference. I have a brainwave. I know that we cannot have any outside visitors into the home, but the Three Amigos may be able to help. They are sitting in the day room chatting over cups of tea.

“Hello there ladies,” I greet them. “So what is the story here? How are things?”

“Fine Angie, we are just chatting about who was the most handsome out of Frank Sinatra, Dean Martin or Cary Grant,” Gloria replies.

“Well, I would not throw Cary Grant out of bed I’ll tell you that for nothing!” Mary chips in.

“We know dear, there’s only one problem with that though,” Betty laughs.

“What, what may I ask is the problem with that?” Mary is laughing indignantly.

“You are not his type and of course there’s your dodgy hip that’d be no good for staying or throwing! He would definitely go for me!” Betty pouted and flounced her hair dramatically.

“You only wish! You are deluded!”

“Ladies I have something to ask you,” I manage to get a word in. “I know that you have all been involved in variety shows in your younger years and I wonder if you might consider what we could do to create a bit of fun in The Beeches now that we have restrictions in place.

Now, we do have some limitations on what may be possible, but I know that the three of you will have some good.”

"You have definitely come to the right place for ideas," Gloria says, "We are the pure definition of fun, you can rely on us."

The Three Amigos cluster together and are delighted that they have the mission of injecting some laughter into The Beeches. This is creating a lift for them and hopefully will lift others, including me.

The day flies from morning into the afternoon and I bump into Niamh in the corridor outside the administration office. I decide to share my idea with her and hope that this is not going to rattle her into a bad mood.

"Niamh, do you have a moment? I know that we are all under terrible stress right now and I have been trying to think of a way to bring a bit of joy back into The Beeches while we are dealing with all these restrictions."

Niamh looked up with interest, "Angie we need as much positivity as we can get at the moment, what do you have in mind?"

"All the staff are seeing the impact that the lockdown is having on our residents. As I see it, the residents are in two groups. We have those who have different stages of dementia, and we need to find ways to 'keep them with us' and remind them of their loved ones as much as we can. Then we have those residents who are with us because they need support and are unable to live independently."

Niamh nods her assent. As I look at her, I can see that the worry of the pandemic has etched it way onto her features. There are faint lines around her eyes I have not noticed previously, and her forehead is set with a slight frown.

I continue, "I have asked Gloria, Mary and Betty to come up with something to entertain the other residents. You see, they really are feeling the lack of the dancing and singing, and I wanted to keep them busy and diverted with creating something. I do not know what it might be, but they are plotting as we speak."

"That is a great idea, cannot wait to see what they come up with!" Niamh declares. A smile is given readily, and she carries the files in her arms into the office.

Result! I have a seal of approval from the steely Niamh. Now I must hope that the Three Amigos will produce the goods. The distraction will keep them busy at least.

Chapter 13

At the end of the shift, I pack up and walk out of the door ready to put my thinking cap on for other things I might be able to do. I can think of nothing, but then again ... nope still nothing. I see Mick walking in front of me with an elaborately dressed Leo, this time sporting a fetching red jumper. I walk a little faster to catch him. By the time I am level with him I am a little puffed, my breath feeling sharp and catching in my throat.

"Hey Mick! It's me!" my words are half gasps.

"Angie! Howya! Was meaning to call, how is my ma doing? How's she looking?"

"She's ok Mick, not quite her usual bright and breezy self. She is missing her visits from you. It is so hard on all the residents. I am trying to think of ideas that may give them a bit of a lift but drawing a blank at the moment."

Mick screws his eyes up and I can almost see the thoughts flying across his face as he considers options for helping residents and families.

"I'm sure you've all thought of Skype and Facetime," he offers.

"There's been some talk of that yes, I guess that's getting the technology in place, but a promising idea," I say. "I think that it would be a clever way to find a way of knitting them back into the broader community as well, we have so many people who normally visit the home other than family, it would be nice to introduce a way of keeping that feeling going. You must remember that some of them do not even have family to visit either because they live abroad or there is no one, not everyone is as lucky as Breda."

This is not easy and with all the restrictions in place for everyone it is hard to even reach out to the community. This looks as though it is going to be a strong cup of tea problem to solve.

I walk back towards Grove House with Mick.

Once back home I grab a quick bite to eat and then make that strong cup of tea. The challenge to arrive at something that will entertain and connect people. I turn the news on, and I see a story about older people cocooning in their own homes and neighbours checking in on them. I smile as this is the system we have in place in Grove House however, I think that it will soon be time for me to take a backward step from that arrangement to protect the others; residents and staff of The Beeches and of course myself.

There is a knock at my door, and I open it to Ursula, dressed in a vibrant purple dress with a lilac scarf tied stylishly at her neck. She could be an advertisement for how to age gracefully with not a hair out of place and her nails short but beautifully manicured. She has an envelope in her hand.

"Angie, Mick tells me that you are looking for ideas to help cheer up the folks down at The Beeches, I think this might be an answer!" She waves the envelope in my face, and it fans a faint coolness on my cheeks as she does so. I step back from the waving envelope with a puzzled look on my face.

"How about asking the local schools to write to residents like old fashioned pen pals?"

"I'm not sure we will be able to take letters in like that Ursula, we are being very restricted at the moment in relation to things coming in from outside."

"Hmmm, I see, but maybe Sinead might know one of those clever technology ways of dealing with things." Ursula is not going to let this idea go easily.

"I'll go and give her a knock now and see what she thinks!" Ursula turns on her heel and is across the landing in double quick time, responses attuned by years of quick-fire salsa.

"Sinead my lovely are you there pet? I have a question of a technical nature to pose for you and I think that you are just the girl to sort it out for me." This is a tenacious

Ursula before me, and I hope that Sinead has an answer that Ursula will like!

Ursula appraises Sinead of the situation and at the end of the stream..."Old fashioned pen pals.... cannot just send things in for fear of the COVID...what can be done to deal with this so that those poor aul folks get to feel as though someone is bothered about them....so what do you think Sinead, is it there something to be done?"

A single word of an answer, "Yes."

"Did you say yes pet? Really it is that easy, just, yes?" Ursula is positively glowing with the thought that her vision can be realised. I am extremely interested to hear what this solution is.

Sinead continues, "It could be pretty straightforward really depending on who is going to be doing the 'letter writing.' If it is going to be school children, you could approach local schools with the idea. All the schools are out at the moment, but the teachers will still be in touch with their pupils, and they could send an email to the parents asking who would like their children to be involved."

"But how would that be the solution?" Ursula asks.

"Once the school, or schools, and the parents have agreed, then the children could be assigned a writing or drawing project and their parents could photograph the letters or pictures, send them into the teacher and then they could be emailed to The Beeches. I think that would probably cover any concerns about infection and the safety of the children."

Ursula and I look at Sinead in admiration. This does sound like an elegant potential solution, and I hope that Maureen and Niamh will think that it is a good idea. On top of the solution, Sinead also offers to help with any of the tech side of things to make it work. I thank the ladies profusely; this could be a great answer to bringing a bit of normal back to the lovely residents.

I return to my flat and as I sit down on the sofa my mobile phone pings at me. I lift it and see a message has arrived from Maureen. This does not look good; she makes a point of not disturbing staff when they have finished shifts. I open the message and read...

"To the Care Team

I am sorry to say that we have had it confirmed that we have our first case of COVID 19 at The Beeches. We will need to implement new work and care protocols in line with HIQA and NPHET[6] guidance..."

The text continues and outlines new working schedules and PPE requirements. Any thoughts of introducing 'in house' activities at The Beeches cannot proceed and I know that this is going to make things even more challenging for us all to deal with. Many of our residents are hard of hearing, and this is going to be a nightmare when they normally watch our lips as we are speaking to them. Masks stop this facial contact and create another break in connection.

I know that in some ways I am lucky that at least I live on my own, but the messages come in thick and fast from the other carers who are at home with families. They are terrified of taking the virus back to their loved ones and all the staff are reading stories of people stripping off outside their family homes to not take the virus in on their clothing. I take a deep breath and look at my moon cactus Luna. I need to think all this through very carefully as I genuinely do not want to put any of my fellow cactus growers at risk. I think back to the contact I have had in the past day. The recent exchange on the landing was distanced, but I cannot be sure that I do not

6 National Public Health Emergency Team, Ireland

have the virus myself and furthermore, if I have inadvertently passed it on to Mick, Ursula, or Sinead.

The images of coffin-filled churches in Northern Italy fill my head. I run through Maureen's message again. One resident in the home has contracted COVID. How did that happen? It could only have been brought in by one of my colleagues, there are no other visitors coming in. I try to think if any of the others had said that they felt ill, but hadn't I read somewhere that it is possible to have the virus and be asymptomatic? How are ordinary people supposed to manage this sneaky insidious illness?

I send a message into the Grove House chat group Sinead has set up.

"Hi everyone, unwelcome news I am afraid, I have just heard that one of the residents at work has got COVID. I wanted to let you know because I just received notification and I am going to have to get tested. I am hoping that firstly I have not got the virus, and then if by some awful chance I have, that I have not passed it on. I would be lying if I did not say that I am quite scared for myself and for all of you. Take care of yourselves and please stay safe, A x."

The messages came back.

"Angie don't worry let's keep everything crossed that you are OK. Let me know if there is anything I can do to help you, Tom."

"Oh Angie, sorry to hear that news I know that you are being so careful with minding yourself. I am happy to do anything I can to help, Mick."

"Angie, that's scary all right, but fingers crossed you will be fine when you get your test. No point in worrying about something until it has happened. God Bless, Ursula."

"Right Angie, sorry to hear that news. Ursula is right, let us wait for the result and see what happens. In the meantime, I can help you get sorted in relation to shopping and anything else you need. I am sure you are going to be rushed off your feet from what I have been hearing and seeing on the news. We are here for you, S."

I feel the tears welling up in my eyes. This little group of neighbours who banded together over a clearance of rough ground and then blossomed into the Cactus Growers' Club are wrapping their good wishes around me like a fuzzy comforter and I am so incredibly grateful. Their kindness is overwhelming, and they do not miss a heartbeat in their offers of support. I hope that they stay well; I think that my heart will break if one of them falls ill.

Another text from Maureen,

"Hello everyone, a further update. There will be a staff briefing in the morning about the new protocols being introduced because of the infection. PPE will be in sealed bags labelled with staff names for when you arrive here tomorrow. Mind yourselves and see you in the morning. Maureen."

I nearly put the news on the television but stop myself. The constant deluge of information is dragging me down. I know that this is serious, for goodness sake it is now knocking on the door of the place where I work, and I am having to get tested. Do I really need any more announcements? I am terrified as it is. I cannot consume any more doom and gloom. As Ursula says, cross that bridge when I come to it. I see the pile of affirmation cards next to Luna. I pick up the top card and turn it over. The words are particularly apt, 'You never know how strong you are until being strong is the only choice you have,' apparently Bob Marley said that.

"Do you know Luna I think that Bob is right, I know that I am resilient, and I am going to get through this. It is not going to be easy, but I am going to succeed." I silently thank Paula for the gift of these little nuggets of optimism and start humming "Three Little Birds" with the refrain don't worry about a thing.

Another message comes through about testing procedures tomorrow and tiredness hits me like a tsunami. My head sinks into the pillow and I do not even hear the familiar night-time noises from the zoo through my open bedroom window. The mist of worry is covering everything around me.

Chapter 14

What can I say about work?

When I arrived this morning, the atmosphere had changed as if charged by a nervous energy that infects everyone in The Beeches. I discover that the resident who has the confirmed case of COVID is Moira, our walking with purpose lady with early-stage dementia. This is not good news, her regular visitations around to other areas of the home means that she could easily have spread the virus quite widely. The next discovery about how COVID came into the home is a call received by Niamh from the plumbing firm who have the contract with The Beeches. It is to say that the plumber who had been called in to work on a leak in the past week and a half, had been tested and confirmed with the virus. The leak had been in Moira's ensuite. The unravelling begins.

In the staff room there is a station set up with packs of PPE for all the staff working my shift. The protective equipment comprises masks and layers of aprons we must wear over our regular uniform. One of the packs has Camilla's name on it but she has not arrived for work today. Maureen says that Camilla has phoned in and is feeling unwell with a feverish temperature and pounding headache and is waiting to be tested again for COVID. Camilla is the first member of staff to be presenting with any symptoms. I pause to think about the last time I was rostered with Camilla or had been working in close proximity, I know that sounds selfish and goodness knows I feel guilty for even thinking like in this way, but this is all way too close and I excuse myself that it is only natural that I feel vulnerable.

As I put on the protective clothing, I am conscious of myself morphing into an alien with the mask and all the additional layers of plastic dermis. It is hot and uncomfortable in the warm atmosphere of the care home, and I have only had the additional layers on for a few minutes. I dread to think how I am going to feel after a few hours of working my shift in this get up. Goodness only knows how we appear to the residents! They are already confused and scared and some really do not understand what is happening and why things have changed so dramatically. I grab a sheet of paper and print my name on it in capital letters and draw a smiley face beneath the letters. I tape the paper to the front of my plastic apron; the residents may not be able see my face, but they will know who I am and that I have a smile for them.

Maureen told us earlier that when a resident is a confirmed COVID case, they will not be admitted to hospital and will have to remain in the home. I am staggered at this news, we are not equipped to deal with serious illness here, however the hospitals are already struggling with infection rates and there is an embargo on transfers. I remember from my nursing days that there are many infection protocols hospitals can put in place when there is a contagious breakout, but this is a residential home not a hospital. This is a place of social care and I do not know how we will be able to keep our people safe.

The older part of the house has been repurposed rather than designed in the same way as a hospital. As Niamh says, it is reassuring to know that it was not a member of staff who brought the virus into The Beeches however, there is no comfort in the fact that it may have now spread through the staff and other residents. We must relocate Moira to another room in the building and a deep clean of her old room is undertaken. She does not understand what is happening and her condition is deteriorating quickly. Even in a short period of time her breathing is becoming laboured, and she is struggling to eat or drink. Two members of the care team, Martina and Kim, are allocated to work with Moira and cannot be allocated to other duties in the home to try to reduce the risk of cross-contamination. Food and clean linens are left at the door to her room and no one else is permitted to enter or work with her. It is lonely work for the hours of the shift and of course, it also creates additional pressure on everyone working in the home as we are all taking on additional duties. There are no complaints, we all know that we must work through this situation and help each other as much as we can. The staff are COVID tested, but there are delays in the results of the tests being returned and for some time we all feel as though the sword of Damocles is hanging over us. In the time between the test happening and getting the result I feel as though I am in a growing no man's land. I cannot be near any of my neighbours, and I wear a mask everywhere. Trying to buy masks for personal use outside work is nearly impossible. We do have them for work but that's it; they are strictly for work, and we have to source anything extra for our own use by ourselves.

Each day I come home from work I feel as though I am in a real life 'The Elves and The Shoemaker' story. My neighbours leave me gifts at my door. The first day there were flowers from Ursula. The second day, a box of facemasks and hand sanitizer from Sinead. On day three Mick left me two beautiful muffins and a box of posh tea. Day four, a homemade bolognese sauce and a pack of spaghetti from Tom. I am deeply moved by these gestures of kindness and thoughtfulness.

After four days I receive my test result and it is negative! I can barely believe the relief when I hear this. The shroud of worry dissipates slightly as I process this. At least for now I am not infected and with a little bit of luck and a lot of caution, I will do my utmost to stay that way. I send a message into the Cactus Growers' WhatsApp.

"Negative!"

The replies come back quickly.

"Hooray," and "Fantastic News," from everyone. Then a tentative question from Mick.

"Who fancies a socially distanced cup of tea in the wilderness?" We all laughingly refer to our reclamation project as the wilderness reflecting its initial state. The "yes" replies come back, but I remind them all to wear masks as they head down the stairs, we do not want to snatch defeat from the jaws of victory!

Cups of tea and coffee in hands, we emerge with our masks into what had been our wilderness. I am amazed to see the transformation, truly the elves have been working outside as well as leaving gifts at my door.

The sight that greets me is nothing short of a spectacular transformation. Where there were once weeds there are now large containers overflowing with the bulbs we had planted. Mick and Tom have made benches and a table with the pallets donated by Mick's friend. The pallets have been sanded and painted in pastel colours and have cushions scattered on them in pinks, greens, and yellows. In the middle of the backrest on each bench there is a stencil of a cactus. It is hard to take it all in and I try to work out when all this work could have been done without me knowing about it. Then again, I guess it would not have been so hard. The rest of my housemates have truly been in lockdown and had been hungering for something to keep them busy and distracted. This space is like an oasis. Solar lights are wrapped around the trunks of the trees and although it is still too light for them to flicker into life at the moment, I can imagine them sending their gentle light over the benches and offering respite from the evenings still to come. I choose a perch away from the others and keep my mask in place other than to take a sip of tea.

What I have not noticed is that Sinead has joined us outside. I glance quickly at Mick who nods gently. No one needs to say anything, we all realise what a big step this is for Sinead. I get the impression there was no way she was going to let this pause for celebration get past her. It is a strange thought that out of all of us, she has adapted to the way of living in times of lockdown in the best way. She adjusted a long time ago to her own enforced indoor living and developed coping mechanisms to deal with the world from the domain of her own sitting room. Sinead is teaching the rest of us how to manage, how to embrace technology to help us and in turn, I like to think that we are helping her find her way back into the world.

"Angie, we have some news," Tom says. "We have gone ahead and contacted some of the local primary schools and they have said that they would be delighted to help with the letter writing for the residents in The Beeches."

"Oh, my goodness, when did you organise this guys? It will be fantastic, thank you, thank you so much!" I exclaim. "This will be a wonderful treat for everyone, thank you."

They fill me in on what the schools have said they will do. The classes from junior infant through to first class are going to make pictures, and the older classes will write letters and stories; the images will be emailed to The Beeches. The schools have also offered to organise recordings of their children singing to send as well. This band of neighbours have reached out to make a difference and by the sounds of it, they are not stopping with the letter writing. While I have been working extended hours and trying to ensure I am socially distanced from everyone, my neighbours, this group of cactus growers, have been looking at things they can do to make small differences.

Ursula is working with her Tai Chi class to make masks for the homeless. She proudly informs me that they have already made three hundred masks and are distributing them through two homeless charities. She says that she was moved to do something when she heard me talking about how hard it is to get masks even in the Home, and then saw Jim sitting with two other homeless men in the Phoenix Park.

“I just got to thinking to myself, how are they going to manage? They are most vulnerable anyway without a place of their own and I wondered what I can do to help.” Her face is earnest with the need to do something beyond herself.

The energy Ursula usually deploys with all the activities she pursues, must surely need an outlet. There is only so much flat-bound salsa she can do before seeking a meaningful reason to stay connected with the others; the co-ordination of the mask makers gives her such a reason.

Ursula then regales us with the story of one of her Tai Chi group, Joan, who has been making masks but constantly varies the design such that the others have to remake her work. I get the sense that Ursula might prefer Joan to hang up her mask-making efforts but is too kind to say that aloud.

The search for a purpose or contribute is one of the things I hear most frequently on the news and social media. Everyone is trying to make some sense of themselves and their lives, in the face of this faceless pandemic. As well as Ursula pitching in with mask making, Tom is lending a hand by making deliveries of the finished masks; he says that his years with Dublin Bus mean he is born to manage logistics!

I take a deep breath and say, “Folks this is the last time I think that I am going to be able to meet up with you for a while, I was reluctant to come down now, but given that I had a negative test, and we are well away from each other then I decided to take a chance. COVID is at The Beeches and I dread bringing it home to you all so I will be keeping a low profile. I am going to deeply miss our chats in person but maybe we can do that online instead, until this thing is more under control?”

They all look at me and I know that they appreciate the gravity of my message. I am very much a risk and I do not want to put them in danger. We talk through the sort of measures that are being advertised by the Health

Executive. Masks, handwashing, sanitiser, social distancing. Isolation.

Sinead speaks, “Angie, if nothing else I consider myself something of an expert in being alone and staying away from people. I will organise to put things in place for you here to help, we will get a regular online chat going so that you have a chance to let off steam. We could even have an online dance class with Ursula or a virtual cookery session with Mick. There are loads of things that we can help with to keep you company without actually being in your company.”

Six months ago, I did not know this woman nor this group of neighbours and now they are all linking together to form a human lifeline while I enter a bubbled ‘never world’ of work and home. There are so many things that I had hoped to do and have looked forward to, including the visit that Paula has not been able to make. I think of a quote that I read recently, ‘You can’t go back and change the beginning, but you can start where you are and change the ending’[7]. These words are resonating with me; I can be sorry for myself and even question why I moved away from the familiar, but that will not get me anywhere, and no one could have anticipated this dreadful virus sweeping across the entire world. I say a thankful and thoughtful goodbye

7 C.S. Lewis

and head back up to number 4. I wipe the handles of the doors with antiseptic spray as I head back to my flat, a practice I will make a constant. I get back to the first floor and to my castle and my cell while all this continues.

My phone pings with a WhatsApp message.

"The Cactus Growers' Club – cook-along with Mick. Tuesday evening. Don't worry Angie we will leave the ingredients outside your door; you will not have to do anything except join in!" From cactus growing to cooking, my emotional support network is once again working their magic.

Chapter 15

Moira died. I discover this when I arrive for my shift a week after she was diagnosed with COVID. After the virus was confirmed, her health deteriorated quickly and, like a light being switched off she is gone, not a flicker and not a pause. Her conscious mind had left before her, taking with it all the memories of the woman she had been from youth to marriage, to motherhood and beyond, blazing a trail for her departed body to follow. Moira had been a gentle person gifted with a kind disposition, her dementia had led her back to younger days where she dwelled until there was just too much fog gathering and obscuring where her girlish memories remained. The memories that informed her of who she was and what she wanted to be were impossible to access. Her walking with purpose was part of her trying to find a physical way back to clarity. Now there is no more seeking, just the stop.

There can be no funereal gathering and marking of this life. Her family are not permitted into The Beeches and the restrictions that are now in place do not allow the normal Irish way of mourning and of celebrating a life lived well; just ten people are able to gather to say that final goodbye. It is not possible to even have a physical book of condolences for the family to hold and to read. Martina had kept a diary of Moira's last days and this will be given to Moira's family; a gesture of the final days that had been contained and shielded from the rest of the Beeches as well as we could manage. Her room had been shrouded with a temporary awning outside her room so that her carers could change into and out of their protective clothing as they started and finished work. Martina was one of her care team and shares her sadness and fear of the impact of COVID. She normally lives at home with her own mother who has underlying health issues and has moved in with one of the other members of the team to avoid potentially infecting her mam.

I do not know anyone who is not feeling the stress of exposure to an extent. The government is acknowledging the fact that care workers are part of the front-line provider group, but I am not sure that the rest of the world are seeing us quite like that. The coverage of the hospitals, with nightly announcements of the number of patients in intensive care, is at the forefront of the minds of the viewers, us not so much.

After receiving the news that the PPE is going to be exhausted in the next few days, I head in to see Mick's mam Breda. She is very sullen and barely glances when I enter the room.

I greet her, "Good morning, Breda how are you today?" I try to be as upbeat as possible.

"Which one are you then?" she replies, knowing full well that I am the only English member of the staff, and my accent sticks out like a sore thumb.

"Ah now Breda have a guess! I know it's not easy with these masks on but surely you can recognise me all the same?" I tease her a little, but I know she is a little hard of hearing and always relied a bit on being able to see my lips to read them. That option has well and truly been removed and now it is a ping pong match of comments followed by "What!?!"

I speak louder, "Breda, its Angie! How are you getting on today?"

I laugh at the reply, "Well, I've still got me legs, that's for sure, not that they are much use to me, but they're still there!"

"Better than not having them at all!" I retort.

"Do you know something Angie my age does not bother me, but I hate all the side effects!" Breda exclaims.

I think to myself that is a truth that we all should get our heads around as we grow older. I am sure that if any of us could chat to our twenty-year-old selves we would counsel ourselves to appreciate how good we are, rather than to be critical about being too fat, too thin, too tall, too short, too anything because however we are in our youth that will be our best.

Breda is growing tearful. Her face is a cross hatch of wrinkles that are now so deeply set they are pathways of all the emotions she has experienced in her long life. Her eye lines, normally telling of laughter expelled, now serve as conduits for her tears as they roll down her cheeks. I feel helpless that I am not able to comfort her with a hug, that uncomplicated way of transferring kindness and positive energy from one person to another and to say everything will be alright without speaking. These human touches are forbidden in our unfamiliar environment and so I can only try to make her feel a bit better with my words.

"It is so difficult Breda, we are all feeling it, but have a little look here... Mick has sent me some photos of Leo to show you. I take out my phone and although I cannot pass it over to Breda, I am able to enlarge the images so that she is able to see her beloved pooch after she perches her glasses on the end of her nose.

“Would you ever look at the wee pet! He is my little man, I miss him so much. There is nothing like the devotion of a dog. He would sit on my lap at home and fall asleep on me at least until someone had the audacity to approach the front door and then he was the fiercest guard dog in the world.”

The image of Leo being fierce is a mental picture I can conjure very easily. He is singular in his bad temper, and I do not like him too close to my ankles when I meet him with Mick. Breda’s description of him as a lap dog is inconsistent with his day-to-day tutu terrorising.

Breda asks how Mick is managing and what life is like outside. This is a totally cocooned world she is now living in, and I know that she is worried about her son. I talk willingly about Mick and the other neighbours in Grove House. Breda is happy that he is surrounded by people who are all looking out for each other and seems comforted that he has been able to continue working in the café. There is little point in talking about the rest of the world. The news and updates seem to be on a relentless loop and that is not really helping anything other than societal ennui and panic. To focus on the local and domestic is the right way to go and this is the conversational space where I choose to stay.

After our chat and a restorative cup of tea – along with a secreted contraband biscuit - Breda is in better form. I am hopeful that we can keep her safe for Mick so at least there is some prospect of them seeing each other in person in the not-too-distant future. I say that I am hopeful, but there is a niggling part of me that is stamping caveats all over that thought.

Chapter 16

The passage of time takes peculiar twists and turns and is moving at a new and unsettling pace. I feel as though life is like a suspended animation and yet everything is still moving forward. I still age, I ache, I move and I work. My world has become shrink-wrapped with restrictions and physical barriers and every activity beyond the basic is met with the resistance of a vacuum sealed package. I am constantly masked, sanitised and away, removed from others. Days bleed from one into the next with time being marked only by new rosters and television series. The shroud of COVID has brought a dystopian atmosphere to the streets around me. People are fearful of each other and the oppression of the pandemic. Even the green lung of the Phoenix Park cannot pump oxygen into the oppressive atmosphere charged with fear of this unseen marauder. Everyone I encounter is trying to dress their lives in normality but none of this is even vaguely normal. To be honest with you I am not sure that I would really know normal anymore and if it came knocking, I think that I would be rather intimidated by it.

Society is exposed to celebrity offerings of online fitness, wellness, or latest crime drama. There is a sense of common experience I cannot remember since watching television shows like Morecambe and Wise in the 1980s. New programming is limited because it is not possible to make large scale dramas so there are plentiful repeats and news; just so much news all the time. It does not matter what we watch and what we do there remains an enormous elephant in the room, living and thriving, with the pandemic forming its outline. It is hard to escape from the dark cloud of the latest numbers of those who have died from the virus and the constant references to the numbers in ICU. There is no theatre, there are no concerts or live music. Artistic experience is contracting like an inward breath that is impossible to exhale, suffocating and fallow. Internet streaming services are viable alternatives to all the other television channels with recommendations being requested and responded to via social media as well as the rare mask to mask interactions.

Masks of all types and colours and styles are now everywhere; a common place accessory presenting everyone with an anonymity that we all accept, legislate and mandate for. The face coverings are creating income opportunities for those who are happy to make them, and the internet is alive with cottage mask industries selling their wares. From milliners to clothing designers, the masks are made and sold in places from local pharmacies to online marketplaces. It is a sellers' market as the weeks go on and there are no signs of the relaxation of rules and people seem accepting of what is happening. News reports are beginning to introduce coverage of those who do not agree with masks and are mounting marches to object to restrictions. I am a pretty laissez faire person in normal circumstances, but I find the marches extremely hard to understand. Yes, life is very different, and it is not an easy environment to navigate, but then I think of all the residents I have been caring for and the very challenging circumstances we are working through. I think of Moira and her family who have been denied the chance to see her or to mark her life as they would have wished. I think of the layers of protective clothing we must wear during a twelve-hour shift. I think of the restrictions I have personally put around myself to protect my friends and neighbours. However, there is no point in me worrying about what others are doing, I am only one and I can only be responsible and accountable for my own actions.

The 2-kilometre distance restrictions in place mean that the local walkers are more frequent and more visible, rolling along against a background of waves of painted rainbows in the windows of family homes. The rainbows are a thank you and declaration of acknowledgement of frontline workers and the service they are giving to society. There are large and small rainbows in arced multicoloured undulations framing my route to work and towards the entrance to the park; I think that it would be nice to find a crock of gold at their end, but more likely to be a litre of milk in the corner shop! Walkers track along the pavements outside Grove House as they take their daily, sometimes twice daily, constitutionals. When I am not working, I watch the walkers from my window seeing them disappear and reappear from their outings to the park, some alone, some in family groups mustering young children on scooters and bicycles. The children's voices are bright trills of fun as they head towards the park. They are watched by young peers grasping crayons and marker pens occupied by the colouring until they can break free on their own walking adventures with their parents, thankful for the distraction that the artwork brings while they are trying to maintain their jobs via Zoom meetings. Thank goodness for technology, delivering the possibility of working in a way that could not have happened only a few years ago. Now businesses, families, and friends are zooming through to the sitting rooms and bedrooms and any rooms where the speaker and the listener engage - from corporate decisions to a weekly family quiz.

My route to the park takes me past Kiera's store. A perspex box has been constructed around the till area and she sits inside, sealed against the germs that the visiting customers may be bringing with them when they are purchasing their milk and bread. The hand sanitiser stations at the front of the shop and next to the till, stand like sentries with signs sternly stating the required social distancing regulations. Everywhere there are screams of the symptoms to look out for and what to do, yellow, black and white signs are liveried like wasps and declare danger.

As I enter the large grey pillars of the park, I can see Mick's cafe's closed shutters and stroll in the direction of the zoo. I have fond memories of my very first night trying to work out what the noises of the animals were and not realising my proximity to the king of the jungle and his queens. My first night is a world away now and it saddens me to hear that the zoo is under threat of closure because of COVID restrictions and the simple financial fact that there is not enough money to feed and keep the animals. As a result, an online fundraising campaign has started with animal lovers donating from all over the country. I ponder what all the animals might think, going from the normal business of human voyeurs to just the keepers, are they lonely? Do they miss their visitors in the same way the rest of the world are missing people? I imagine the animals vying for their keepers' attention, 'Look at me! Look at me!' By contrast to the zoo animals, the roaming Phoenix Park deer herd have plenty of regular onlookers as they freely graze on the fields of green grass, the closest thing to a savannah that Dublin has to offer. I think it is the nearest I will get to a savannah of any type anytime soon I guess I will have to dream on. I revel in my mini escapes into the open spaces of the park, and I recognise my more relaxed state mirrored in the faces of the others who are walking through their stresses and strains. This gives a different spin on Ursula's 'movement is life' philosophy, movement is mental balance and respite and I embrace all the benefits it has to offer in these outings to this calming space. I reflect, not for the first time, how fortunate I am to live so close to the park rather than in a more concreted part of the city where the only greenery are the weeds poking though cracked paving, I think that I may be a bit cracked myself if that was the only vista available.

We have three confirmed COVID cases at The Beeches. One death so far. Finally, we have the necessary PPE we need to protect ourselves properly, but it still feels a bit like amateur night in the light of what we are dealing with. Maureen is trying to organise the roster against a background of extreme staff shortage and people being out and having to isolate. I know that she is doing her absolute best to try to keep everything going but being scheduled for double shifts is both exhausting and exasperating. I try to get in to see Breda when I am working, but recently I have been rostered in with the COVID residents and that means that I am unable to be anywhere else in the home for the duration of those shifts.

Mick phones me in work to say that he has just heard from Niamh that his mum has tested positive for COVID. He is devastated.

"Jesus, Angie! Is she going to be OK? I am terrified that this will be the end of her. I feel so helpless, no, useless, that's how I feel." Silence then.

"Look Mick I totally understand," I try to soothe him, "we can all only do our best now. I know it will not be much consolation, but if your mum is moving to the isolation area of the home then at least I will be able to see her and look after her myself and I can let you know how she is doing, first-hand so to speak."

"Is that what you are doing now Angie, just the COVID residents? I hadn't realised." Mick is noticeably quiet again. I guess he must be thinking that it is a pretty rough spot to be working in, day in and day out. It is. I feel like a trussed-up chicken most of the time and it is very hard to not be able to move around other areas or even mix with the other staff. I can honestly say that my most significant relationship in recent weeks has been with my cactus, at least there is no danger of passing anything on to it and better yet there is no chastising when I use a lot of swear words to just let off steam!

"Look Mick, you know that I will do my absolute best for your mum and now that she will be moved, I will make sure you at least get to do a video call on Facetime or WhatsApp, it's not a perfect answer but it is something."

"Thanks Angie.... How are you bearing up? I have not seen you recently, what I am saying! Yep, I know we have our rules at home about keeping apart, but you have not even been on any calls recently, I have not even passed you on a walk, are you alright?"

I pause before I answer.

"Mick, this is not easy, you've seen all the news reports. I feel like a zombie heading in and out. Burnt out does not even go near to how I feel. I am heading out for walks, but I need space and time to process what I am dealing with and I am not very good company at the moment. The reason I am still doing what I am doing is for your mum and the other residents at The Beeches and for my colleagues of course, there is no slack that can be picked up by others. There are no more others."

Another pregnant pause in the conversation.

"Right so," Mick says. "Oh Angie I know something that might give you a bit of a lift, did you know that Jim has found somewhere to live with one of the homeless charities? One small upside of all this chaos is that there has been a push to try to get people off the streets to give some sort of protection. He looks as though he might be getting himself together a bit, poor bugger has had a difficult time."

I can feel my eyes welling up with tears. This is a speck of light in a period where the dark has only been getting inkier and deeper. I know that this is not the whole answer, but for Jim just to have a bit of security and hopefully be on a better track, well that is something.

"That is good news, thanks for letting me know, he has been on my mind over the past couple of months and I had not seen him around, was worried that the worse had happened," I did not want to use the word 'died.' We say our goodbyes and I get a call from Niamh to say that Breda is going to be moving to the isolation area with me.

Breda is not in good shape when she arrives. Her breathing is shallow, and her colour has changed from her usual healthy complexion to an icy grey. Her eyes appear sunken into her head and the glimmer of devilment has disappeared.

I greet her, "Hello Breda, my love, it's Angie," I see her eyes try to focus but my PPE camouflage will not allow her to see who I am. I must look like an alien in this get up. All she can see are my eyes, but they are distorted by the curved plastic face shield that sends the outline of my face to abnormal angles, defying recognition. She is receiving oxygen, at least that is something, but there is little we can do for our residents here. This is not an intensive care unit, and I cannot provide full nursing support in these conditions. All I can do is to try to make her comfortable and hope for the best. Speaking softly and trying to soothe her concerns, I settle her into this new room and put her beloved photos of Mick and Leo next to her bed. I honestly do not know what I am going to say to Mick about his mum, any improvement will be pure luck rather than anything else. Hours and days are precious in this situation, I guess they always are but normally there is the natural distraction of day to day living that disguises how fleeting time really is. I know from my own experience that it is only when life is at its hardest that we pause to take stock of all the time we have taken for granted; maybe that is why life is designed in this way so that we do not dwell on the way time runs away with our own mortality, fudging things so that we are in the main slightly distracted.

Dusk creeps outside and my shift ends. I must shed my sheath of PPE in a cordoned off part of the corridor. I would like to say that I am like an emerging butterfly peeling away her chrysalis, but that would be a way too colourful and romantic description of removing masks, gloves and plastic aprons and finally throwing my uniform into a bag that is sealed and then taken to the laundry with the other items of bedding and clothing from this lockdown area. I gaze at my hands that are cracking with the constant wearing of gloves and the incessant application of hand sanitiser and hand washing. They appear wizened and old, somehow out of place at the end of my arms. My hands are the tools of my work and they have been enduring their own tortures while I am trying to help others get through their battles. I dress in my own clothes to head home, once again to change there and to launder what I am wearing now. I think that everyone here should buy shares in detergent companies! Between soaps and washing powder they must be literally 'cleaning up!'

When I arrive home, there is a card under the door. I open it and on the front there is a picture of a kitten dangling from a branch. The words "Hang in there" in a comic typeface underneath. Inside just two words.

"Thanks, Mick."

The waterworks are fully turned on this time. I slump into my sofa and the sobs will not be stifled. Tiredness and the pure overwhelming emotion are just too much. I do not have a good feeling about how Breda is going to fare and do not have the heart to say anything to Mick, I do not think that I would be able to in any event, I am sure there must be rules hidden somewhere in The Beeches operating manual that forbids discussing such things with family members even if they are friends. Only formal channels permitted in these situations, but it is going to be difficult if he asks me directly. I will have to cross that bridge when I come to it.

Chapter 17

There are a lot of prayers incanted at The Beeches. Each following their own God in hoping that things will get better. The reach of the COVID section is growing through the home. Each day we wait for the virus to tap a shoulder, to invite either a resident or staff member into the dance that may or may not prove to be their last.

I think that Mick has been speaking to the others in Grove House. Tokens of affection and support appear outside my door along with the food shopping that is still done as a group activity. Sinead continues to help the others as their tech support person and is almost flourishing in this situation where there is no choice but to remain inside and cocooned from the world. I sense a change in the way she feels about herself in the messages she sends across in the cards she has customised from online card shops. It is true that there is a place and a time for all things; even this place and time. I avoid meeting up with my housemates in person.

Things are just too risky with the way things are in the home and the number of cases rising, but we exchange photos of our cacti and there are even comic shots of the prickly succulents striking poses. Mick sends a photo of “Bugs” next to an empty bag of carrots. Tom snaps “Beryl” with a rolling pin propped up against her. Anything to raise a smile and I suspect this may be mainly for my benefit. Looking at the photos our cactus charges are all growing well, and Ursula sends us messages of congratulations on how well we are tending them. I would never have imagined that I would be getting a well done on the performance of a cactus, but strange times lead to even stranger pastimes. I often think that the bit of control we all have over tending our plants is like saying to the universe this is one spot where all the rubbish happening now cannot encroach and those cacti are sticking up their prickles to the world like their equivalent of the middle finger.

Four days after Breda is moved to the isolation room her breathing deteriorates significantly. There is still no prospect of a move to a hospital which is where she should be treated. Instead, she remains with us, in less than satisfactory circumstances. The advice is to turn patients on to their stomachs when they are truly struggling with their breathing. When we do this for Breda she is as light as a feather, all her body mass has been exhausted in trying to fight off this virus and nothing other than fluids being taken into her weakened body through a drip. I talk to her about Mick and Leo and tell her about the cacti and the snippets of life from outside. She lapses in and out of awareness and I can see some reaction when I speak of her son, the son she adores, who is himself worried sick about what is happening with his beloved mam and not being able to see her. I try to show photos of the grumpy Leo, again a flicker of recognition, but this is not the feisty and formidable woman I met only a few short months ago. I can see her fading quickly, becoming less of herself and less of the world. I sit beside her bed and despite all the rules, my gloved hand takes hers and I hold it as if trying to hold that moment in time. Pushing back what I know will be inevitable and desperately sad.

Breda's breathing is staggered, gasping, one moment stopped and the next rattling. She opens her eyes and looks directly at me. In that moment I think that she does recognise me, and I see a deep fear in her eyes. This is not the final moment of someone who is reconciled to leaving this life. This is the grasp of someone who wants to stay but is being denied that possibility by the conspiracy that is raging through their body and calling time for the last time. The grip loosens and the breath stops and she is gone. The body that once was in its ultimate moments has lost animation and the diminished light inside her has extinguished.

My visor starts to mist as the tears come quietly. Every one of these losses is painful, but this one particularly so, given the friendship I have with Mick. I have no option but to let the tears roll down my face; I cannot wipe them with my gloved hands. I must wait until I can safely remove all the PPE and only then, will the traces of the tears be dabbed away.

After I have safely changed and refreshed my PPE, I contact Maureen to give her the news about Breda and I ask if it will be possible for me to speak to Mick about his mum's death. Maureen agrees, but also gives me the standard information issued to the families of our COVID victims where arrangements are outlined for undertakers and government guidelines in relation to funerals. At least I know that I can talk to Mick about being with his mum in her last moments and he will know that someone was beside her when she made her final journey. The phone call is not an easy one.

"Mick, hi it's Angie, do you have a minute?" I say when the phone is answered.

"Hi Angie, yeah it's fine to talk, what's up?" he replies.

"I'm so sorry Mick, I have sad news for you, it's your mum, I'm afraid she was struggling with her breathing earlier today and it all became too challenging. I was with her holding her hand when the time came. I think she recognised me at the end, and she had her photos of you and Leo at her bedside."

I am thinking, 'keep it together, keep it together Angie.' I feel the tears coming again but Mick needs me to be strong and to be able to answer any questions he has, not a blubbering wreck at the other end of the phone.

Quietly he speaks, "Oh no, oh Mam, no!"

I can barely hear Mick's words. The sense of sadness and loss is palpable in his voice. I realise that there is nothing that I can say now that will bring comfort. This is a time of processing and thinking for Mick. No space for the trite comment. No, 'she has gone to a better place stuff.' The only place he wanted his mum was sitting with him having a cuppa with the dog between them.

"Angie, thank you for letting me know. I hugely appreciate that it was you with Mam in her final moments. I know that there will be things to do, but I cannot really get my head around any of that now. What about things like erm death certificates and that sort of thing? Do I have to do anything?"

"The Beeches has a pack of information for you Mick. The death certificate will be dealt with by the doctor. I am sure that your mum had her wishes on what she wanted for herself and that can all be arranged but please take a moment. You need to be with the loss right now. Time enough and you have had an awful shock. I am so very sorry about your mum. If you want to speak to me at any stage, please do not hesitate to call."

Breda will be another one of the death statistics that will be stated on the news. So many deaths due to this pandemic. What those numbers on the news and in the press fail to consider is the fact that every single one person has a string of relations and friends who are mourning their loss. The abstraction of statistics distances the reports living members of society to just deaths. Then those numbers become all too real for

Mick and all the families of the world who cannot have the luxury of saying goodbye to their loved ones.

This is truly a red-letter day as far as feeling inadequate is concerned. I send messages to Ursula, Sinead, and Tom to let them know what has happened to Mick's mum. Their replies are virtual hugs:

"Are you OK?"

"Oh no that's so terribly sad, poor Mick he will be devastated. How are you doing?"

"That must have been awful for you, so hard to tell Mick as well, he loved his mum so much. Hope you are OK."

I know that they will be reaching out to Mick, but they have also recognised how awfully hard it was for me to lose Breda. I can feel the glow of affection through their texts. Their sensitivity sears through my need to remain calm and the emotions cascade with thoughts of the deaths of my own family members, compounded by being with Breda in her last moments it is as though I have known this group of empathetic souls for many years rather than months. It is a level of connection I had not experienced with my neighbours in England. Absolutely always with friends, but not the people physically closest to my front door. This pulling together evokes a wonderful sense of being a part of something bigger than myself, a sense of community in this cactus wrangling group and that is another thing that is getting me through all the horrible day to day that I face into. Hopefully, Mick will also feel that way when they reach out to him as he wades through his grief.

My dad always thoroughly enjoyed an Irish funeral. He regarded them as a celebration of a life and returned to the country of his birth many times over the years to mark the passing of family and friends. He described the wakes as circling the wagons around those who are grieving and endless cups of tea with plentiful hang (sic) sandwiches and slices of tea loaf and madeira cake. Often a few tots of whisky thrown in for good measure. I have one vivid memory of attending one of these events with my father. A distant aunt had died and dad insisted that I make the journey over with him to pay our respects. It was the eve of the funeral and Auntie was laid out in the good room at the front of the house. The coffin was open, a first for me, and I walked in just ahead of dad. When the door was closed behind me I looked around to try to see Dad, but no Dad was to be seen. The priest was standing next to the coffin and proceeded to start ten decades of the rosary with some ladies I did not know also reciting. I was thrown by this and muttered along myself, but to be honest I could not really remember all the words, having hopelessly lapsed even at that early age. Once the decades had been completed one of the women leaned forward and said rather loudly to the one next to her, "Well God love her she's terribly failed isn't she!"

I was even more astounded to hear the other woman reply, "Yes she's definitely not looking herself."

I bravely peered into the casket and looked at the waxy complexion of this elderly relative and all I could think was, 'of course she looks failed, she's been dead two days.' A point that I think the women may have overlooked in their assessment. That was my first time seeing a dead body. Of course, I have seen many since then. In my line of work it could be considered an occupational hazard. However, the sense of the people coming together to mark a life, the ritual of acknowledgement, breaking bread, even the getting drunk in some cases, are all part of making sure that it is done quickly, addressed rapidly so that the conversations are not about the 'sorry for your loss' for weeks afterwards. I have painful memories of that after losing my aunt. The funeral arrangements took weeks and then I found that people, in the spirit of kindness, would extend their sympathies, but it seemed to last forever. The Irish approach is like removing a band aid, quite intense but somehow the harshest pain is dealt with quickly.

A text message from Mick:

"Hi Angie, thank you again for all you did for Mam today. It's so very sad, but I am comforted to think that she was not alone. I was wondering if you might be able to help me? I need to find something for the undertakers for the burial. All Mam's clothes are at The Beeches, is there any chance you might be able to find something appropriate for me as I am not able to go in?"

The poor man! Not even being able to do that small act of service for his mother. I immediately reply, "Of course, leave it with me, I will organise that for you tomorrow." Kindness is the order of the day.

Chapter 18

Breda's funeral takes place three days after she died. She is dressed in her best navy-blue skirt and blouse that I had collected from The Beeches for her and had laundered before giving them to Mick. There is a hint of herself about her look, but the Breda Mick loved as a mother is not here. Mick has given the funeral directors some of her photographs to tuck into the side of the casket. Her hands are clutching the pastel-coloured rosary beads she had brought back from a pilgrimage to Fatima twenty years previously. She looks peaceful and there is no hint of her desperation for air in the last moments of her life. The restrictions mean that there are only ten people in the church to mark her life. I attend the mass. There are a couple of her friends sitting far apart at the back of the church. Mick is at the front. The word that describes this congregation best is 'meagre.' The priest obviously knew Breda and describes her to a tee.

"Breda was a strong woman with a huge sense of right and wrong. Her son Michael was her pride and joy, and she was never happier than when she could sit with him and enjoy his tales of café life. She did not have an easy beginning and lost her husband when she was only thirty, rearing Michael as a single mum and a hard working one at that. Breda was an animal lover and the other character in her life was her beloved Yorkshire Terrier Leo. She will be sadly missed by all those close to her and we now say a prayer for her eternal spirit."

Lovely words really, nothing too mushy and I think that Breda would approve. I can imagine anything more sentimental would have met with extreme disapproval. I can see Mick's tears rolling down his face, his grief partially covered by the face mask concealing the tremoring chin and the verge of sobbing. The coffin is wheeled out of the church under a cloud of incense that smells of frankincense and myrrh and catches in my throat as the priest passes.

Breda is cremated at Glasnevin crematorium. The hearse takes her on her final journey. Mick invites me to join him in the funeral limousine, I do not really want to go in there still very aware of the risks, but he looks lost in the black interior of the car on his own, so I reluctantly agree. We sit far apart, masked and with the windows open and the breeze ruffling our hair. The crematorium is situated in the historic Glasnevin cemetery and surrounded by the memorials and monuments to Irish history. Thousands are buried in the graveyard and Breda's remains are taken into the crematorium past those already gone. Words are spoken and then she goes on her journey. Mick has chosen to keep his mum's ashes and will collect them in a few days.

I try to think of the right thing to say. The usual meal and remembrance are not possible. The Gravediggers nor any other pub is open. COVID. We decide to head back to Grove House and are surprised to find a sign pinned to the front door.

"Come round to the wilderness, U, T, S." We walk down the side passage and to the back of the building to find Ursula, Tom and Sinead sitting with a trestle table set up with sandwiches, flasks of soup and buns, along with some beer and a couple of bottles of wine. There are also glasses and plates.

Mick appears quite overcome, "Oh you are so very good," he says. "Do you know that my Mam would've loved all this, she was a party girl at heart, and I am sure that she is looking down at this with a smile." His voice cracks slightly as he says these last words.

Tom pats him on the shoulder and invites him to sit down and have something to eat.

“Come on Mick, it’s been a long day for you and I am sure that you have not had anything today. You will have to keep your strength up, this contagion malarkey does not take any prisoners you know.”

Mick nods and takes a sip of the beer Ursula has handed him. The others ask him to tell them stories about his mam. She was some character and soon the tears of sadness make way for giggles at the antics she got up to. One such event was when Breda had been referred to a consultant because she had been having some dizzy spells and had experienced chest pains. The consultant had examined her and her recollection of the events was that he had muttered “Angina” and she said that she had replied “Enjoying it? It’s bleedin’ great.” We laugh and shed tears with Mick. Breda had been the constant and anchor in his life. He stares down into his drink

“It seems strange to think that I am an orphan now,” he says softly. “Mam was a force of nature and always pushed me to be my best. I don’t really know what I am going to do without her.”

Tom sits up straight and pats his hands down onto his thighs with a clap sound.

“I’ll tell you what you’ll do Mick, you will carry on, you will be the man that your mam wanted you to be. She did not raise you to falter, you have this, and you will continue to make her proud, now no more of this 'what'll I do business' do you hear me?"

Mick gently nods his head. He is weary from the emotion of the day and all the burden of stress that has engulfed him during the past months, no business to speak of and no income with an eroding nest egg being whittled away. The worry of Breda's situation has further taken its toll but it is clear that he knows that Tom is correct, and the important thing is to honour his mum in the best way that he can and that is by getting on with things.

Breda had always been one to find the fun in things and I know I am certainly going to miss the chats with her. We chat and laugh and keep an eye on Mick. Leo is finally allowed into the wilderness and uncharacteristically curls up tight at Mick's feet and will not budge. I believe that little dog knows what has happened and this is his way of showing he is missing her too.

I think that I should be better at goodbyes than I am. I have had some experience of them after all.

Chapter 19

Finally, the 2 km restriction rule lifts and it feels as though we are released from gilded cages and able to go a bit further; first 5 km, then the prospect of county-wide travel. The local walkers venture further from their front doors and, as if by magic, the news is filled with reports of beauty spots being inundated with people who have finally been freed from living under restrictions. The Gardai are deployed to stop people blocking roads and the unseasonal good weather brings the young out in their hundreds to go to the beaches along the county Dublin coast, photographed in their partying gaggles. They emerge from their isolated states like May flies taking to the wind and landing on the sandy shores. The DART[8] and buses are thronged with teens carrying their beach towels, sun cream and stashes of booze ready to mingle with old friends and new. Their landing sites become littered with the debris

8 DART – Dublin Area Rapid Transit, the commuter rail system on the coastline of Dublin Bay

of their moments of clustering. Patches of sand are punctuated by portable barbecues, bottle and cans. Councils are petitioned to provide temporary toilet facilities to cater for the influxes. Many of these young people should be settling down to take their final school exams but having been trapped in a cycle of school cessation and online learning, they grab this chance to just be free from the confines of their bedrooms and online learning.

In many ways I would love to be sitting on a beach looking out at the water lapping the shore, however worries run riot through my head about infection spikes and at The Beeches we are still living with the shadow of fear of contamination and losing more of our residents. The health executive revisions to infection management still come through on a regular basis and there is news of vaccines being developed by the large pharmaceutical companies. The irony is, we are now in a different sort of hopeful race, one that means that our residents and us, the carers, will be able to get a vaccine before succumbing to the pandemic. Daily media updates talk about testing and approval processes in the European Union, The USA and the UK. Politicians are using the pandemic as political hobby horses and it is hard to believe that there are still some global leaders who decry the virus, like ostriches sticking their heads in the sand and hoping that it will all go away.

In this environment of pandemic ping-pong, I come to sit in the wilderness, which has become a flowery oasis for my neighbours and me. I am sipping a cup of tea watching the bees settling on the plants that keep appearing. I think that Tom and Ursula are having some sort of 'plant off' as the number of different flowers increases steadily over the weeks. Lavenders, salvias, daisies, astilbes, heathers and things I simply cannot name replace the earlier bulb colour and fill the space with colour and scent. I hold my mug in two hands and bring it up to my face. The sun is dancing through the patterns of the leaves, casting their movement in shadows. I feel as though I could be anywhere in the world, just caught in this moment and relaxing into bathing my senses in this place we created. Mick's voice jolts me back into the here and now,

"Angie? I wonder do you have a moment?" he asks. I smile, shrug and say, "Of course."

"Angie, I have been thinking. Now that we can travel throughout the county, I have decided what I would like to do with Mam's ashes. She always loved the seaside and one of her favourite places in the world was Howth, she was a huge fan of the fish and chips there and when I was a young fella, we would head out sometimes on a

Sunday afternoon and walk the piers. I think that is where I would like to spread her ashes. I was wondering." He pauses. "Well I was wondering if you might come out with me? I think that Mam would like you to be there, and you were the person with her at the end, it would mean a lot to me."

I feel a surge of affection for this man sitting opposite me. He has obviously been giving a lot of thought as to how he wants to say his last goodbye to Breda. I can only say yes of course. We agree that we will go in a couple of weekends time when I have a day off. I decide that I will drive, I still do not fancy clamouring into buses or trains. It is agreed and I feel privileged that Mick has asked me. It is years since I have been to Howth and the trip will bring back memories for me too.

I head back up to number 4 and I see Sinead on the landing. She is a changed woman from the one I met at the end of last summer. Her confidence has sky-rocketed and she now holds her head up and reveals the most beautiful smile.

"Hi Sinead, you look lovely, where are you heading to?" I ask, delighted to see that she is looking so well.

"Thank you!" she blushes, "I am heading out to the wilderness for a chat with Tom, he has said that a number of his friends would like to learn about their smartphones and what they can do with them, so I have decided to help and we are just going to work out how to do it, maybe a socially-distanced gathering outside? It's exciting though! Nice to think that I might be helping some 'silver surfers!'"

"Don't let Tom hear you call him that!" I laugh, "I'm not so sure he would take very kindly to being called a silver anything!"

This is so great to see Sinead getting involved and, more to the point, that what she is doing has value to others and that they tell her so. She has never shared the reasons why her life became so restricted and why she became so scared, but whatever the reasons are they seem to be behind her, or their volume turned so low on her internal speaker that she is able to play a different narrative. I feel quite honoured that I have been able to be a small part of that, ironically the pandemic has given her an opportunity to reset and re-engage in a way that so called normal life had not. One day at a time and one step at a time, that's all any of us can really do now.

I am working an evening shift today. I head to The Beeches, the roads are still quiet, interrupted only by courier vans fulfilling the online consumerism that has replaced real life shops. One, two, three vans pass me with their mercurial livery promising fast and secure delivery. The trees that had shed their leaves over winter are dressed in their foliage, the greenness a way of nature giving the atmosphere a cleanse. The usual routine of PPE, and updates on the status of residents and any changes to requirements. The big news is that Pfizer are going to be manufacturing a vaccine here in Ireland and this news is being met with great enthusiasm and anticipation. The only question on everyone's lips here is "When?" When will this be rolled out and how much longer will we have to go on like this, waiting for the next case and probably the next death? It is like having a key to the solution - just slightly out of reaching of our stretching fingertips - tantalisingly close and frustratingly distant at the same time! Maureen calls on us all to just keep going and be hopeful that the checks and approvals will come through quickly.

The lovely Three Amigos are unwavering in their optimism, even though all their favourite activities have not been on the menu for months. They have an inextinguishable energy, even in the face of what is happening, and can still be heard along the corridors singing their favourite Doris Day songs. 'Que sera sera' ladies 'Que sera sera.'

The residents are all resembling aged hippies, their hair has not been cut or styled since the start of lockdown and we are not allowed to try to trim them back into shape. The ladies are missing their wash, cut and sets and many of the conversations revolve around how nice it will be when Louise can return to deal with their unruly tresses.

The questions continue. When will things get better? When will a vaccine be ready and approved and distributed? When will we see loved ones? That is true for the residents who have not sunk into a blur of day after day of sameness, certainly I see a terrible deterioration in some. One of our residents who is not coping well with the situation is the affable Bill. He has transformed from a twinkly cheerful chappie to a shell of his former self. Even the lilting melodies from his three biggest fans do little to shake him from his malaise, this isolation is not what he signed up for when he moved into The Beeches.

I recount my day to Ursula, Tom and Sinead in the wilderness that evening. We have fallen into a routine of spacing ourselves around the pallet benches, settled on bright jewel-coloured cushions talking or not talking as the mood takes us. Ursula is hoping that she will be able to see her daughter and her grandchildren before the end of the year, it is two years since she has seen them, and this summer was to be the big get-together before COVID struck and cut air travel off. Ironically, it still does not matter if you are down the road, across a county line, across the Irish Sea or the Atlantic, the lack of face-to-face contact has the same impact. Paula's trip is put on the back burner, and we have no idea when it will happen. She keeps quoting one of her affirmation cards to me.

"Once you choose hope, anything is possible[9], Angie," she says. Hope is a powerful ally in these times. I like to think that it has a magical property that will quash all the hurdles. I share this affirmation with Ursula and she nods sagely and agrees. I have every confidence that as soon as it is possible there will be the most wonderful reunion sprinkled with tears and laughter. In the meantime, she continues to make masks, attend online salsa and Pilates classes and of course, tend to her cactus colony. Tom and Sinead's technology project is well and truly underway now. Tom extolls Sinead's patience and the kind way she has been guiding his friends through their technology 'how to' sessions. She is positively glowing at his words of praise and again I reflect on the fact that this extended household of neighbours have been very good for each other in the past months.

Mick arrives with Leo. They are just back from their walk and Mick has news that he will be able to reopen the café on a takeaway only basis. That is at least a chink of hope. Something to do and income coming in, all good

---

9 Christopher Reeve

news. Leo is less bad tempered than he had been, I wonder if he just wants to give Mick some support and not do his usual nippy little dog impersonation. To my utter amazement he even allows Ursula to pet him! Unheard of previously!

The others take their leave and Mick sits opposite me.

"Well Angie, I think, if it suits you of course, that I would like to scatter Mam's ashes this weekend? Would that still be alright with you?"

"It will be an honour to go with you Mick," I reply, "I'd like to be there and I have not been out to Howth since I was a little girl. I was there once during a summer holiday and we went out to visit Ireland's Eye."

We agree to set out the following morning in the hope of missing traffic and parking easily.

Chapter 20

At nine o'clock the following morning we set off. Mick and I are masked in my Golf. Side by side with Leopold Bloom on the back seat wearing a black bow tie. I set my Google Map with Howth as the destination. The route takes us away from the park and around the North Circular Road. The roads are eerily quiet, and my trusty Golf is the only car on the stretch of road for some time. We do not say very much, just the occasional comment about nothing in particular. We pass the entrance to the Technological University with its new edifices visible from the road. Onwards and it is possible to see the Croke Park stadium looming large to our left. Towards Fairview with its skatepark and then on the coast road travelling out past Clontarf. The sea is to our right, a border of water, on our outbound journey to the fishing village of Howth. The density of the city is left behind us as we continue. Joggers, walkers and cyclists are moving their way along the seaside paths taking them away from the city. Outdoor gym machines punctuate their journeys, along with the iconic pale teal wind shelters, standing like curved waves facing towards the water. The road is made in sections of seamed concrete and there is a thurrump, thurrump sound of the tyres passing over the seams as we advance towards the Howth Peninsula.

Leo stands up with his nose against the window. The new sights fascinating him into making happy whines of excitement at the prospect of a new place to visit. The open grass, the fields of St Anne's Park to our left and then the opening, revealing the folly temple before we reach a magnificent carved tree covered in all manner of sea and land wildlife up to the top crested with birds.

"Would you look at that!" Mick exclaims. "That is amazing, some amount of work went into doing that, we might stop off on the way back to have a better look?"

I agree that it would be great to stop and take in all that work, and we continue towards our destination. The traffic is getting busier as shoppers are heading out to get groceries and others like ourselves are heading to the seaside village of Howth for a visit. Onwards we go and can see the Hill of Howth before us, rising away from the sea, houses winding up the hill like trimming on a tree, wrapping around with highlights of white and creams. We pass through Sutton and then onwards to Howth village itself. This place has an air of being more remote from the city than it really is. Only twelve kilometres in distance but a world away in the look of the place and the greenness around us. The houses lining the road are large with spacious gardens and periodically there are new looking blocks of apartments with sea views. The journey reminds me of that holiday from years before, certainly not an image appropriate for this particular trip but it is a feeling that I simply cannot get away from.

We pass the large gateway that marks the entrance to Howth Castle on our right which is juxtaposed against a derelict industrial site on our left. The aged entry to the demesne appears incongruous opposite building site hoardings, the two places might as well be on opposite sides of the world! Finally, we arrive in Howth village and Mick sits with container Breda's ashes held carefully on his lap. Leo has a sense that this car journey is concluding and gets very excited, desperate to stretch his legs and go and explore all the sights, sounds and smells this new place has to offer.

One of the first things I notice is the sheer number of seagulls, there seem to be hundreds of them; and they are huge! The fishing boats are a great lure for them, and they have obviously worked out there are easy pickings from the visitors who sit along the walls eating their fish and chips. The air is alive with their squawks and calls. There is a slight breeze and the sounds of movement from the harbour where the yachts are moored.

"Well Mick, what do you think? Will we take a walk long the pier here?" I ask. I know that Mick needs to take the lead and decide when and where he wants to say goodbye to his mam. He lifts Leo out of the car and we walk slowly down the first pier. We pass more gulls prospecting for tasty morsels and past restaurants offering takeaway meals, then fishmongers with their specials listed on the blackboards outside the shops. The windows are a veritable feast for the eyes with a huge variety of fish and shellfish as you can imagine, glassy eyes staring out from beds of ice. There are several customers heading in early to purchase their dinners for tonight. We continue to walk and head over to look at the water. There is a ripple and a splash and before our eyes a large seal appears and swims parallel to us as we make our way towards the end of the pier. It is a huge animal, glistening grey with mottles on its underbelly, another wildlife customer who clearly enjoys the bounty of living in a fishing port. We pass a group of ladies walking the pier holding their takeaway coffees and chatting as they move, not unlike their park counterparts on the other side of the city; the need to meet and mix is a universal language.

Towards the end of the pier, we have a choice - we can either continue straight over cobbles or bear round to the right to walk out on the harbour wall. Mick makes the decision for us, and we walk straight ahead. There are stone blocks just low enough to use as makeshift seats and we take a moment to look out across the sea. The breeze is creating wavelets in the water and the sun is putting in an appearance to create shimmers on the surface; ethereal pinpoints of light flitting to and fro.

"Mam loved it here," Mick said looking at the cannister of ashes, "she would have been the first to get the poke of chips and then a ninety-nine ice cream cone, it seems right that we say goodbye here." He pats the cannister.

"I love you Mam and I miss you more than I can say, you always believed in me and gave me the best start any son could have. You will always be with me and I promise that I will look after Leo as long as he lives." He looks at me and hands me Leo's lead to hold.

Mick loosens the top of the cannister and walks to the edge of the pier.

"God bless you Mam, I love you," he crouches and scatters the ashes carefully and they are lifted slightly on the breeze and waft away over the water, like a dream fading. Mick lets out a sigh and wipes a tear from his eye. I walk over to him and stand next to him. He reaches out and takes my hand and squeezes it and I squeeze his hand in return.

Epilogue

The Irish COVID vaccination programme for the elderly residents and carers in care homes commenced in January 2021. There are 580 nursing homes in Ireland with 70,000 living and working in them.

Acknowledgements

I have to say thank you to a number of people who have supported me on the journey to writing The Cactus Growers' Club.

Firstly, I must extend a huge thank you to Karen Stanley, the creator of The Write of Passage Growth Academy. Karen has inspired five first time writers, including myself to embark on a writing journey during this awful pandemic and has also been so generous to me with her time in giving advice and her editing skills.

I am so grateful to Karen, Beverley, Fiona, Jackie and Sandra for sharing this journey. It has long been an ambition of mine to write a book and this ambition has been supported by the creativity and community I have found in the group of first-time writers

Also, many thanks to Karen's new publishing label Mabel & Stanley for accepting my book, I am so delighted to be a part of this exciting new venture.

A huge thank you to my wonderful husband David for reading drafts, editing, offering advice and being so supportive. Thanks also to my children Amy and Andrew who have been great sounding boards. To my Mum and Dad, you are as ever the most wonderful parents, thank you for listening to me as I talked through plot options.

Thank you to Steve at DunWrite Author Services for all the help with formatting and the final look of the book, it would have been a tricky process to navigate without you.

I would like to say a special thank you to AB for your insights into the life of care homes during the pandemic. I am indebted to you for your help and for taking the time to talk to me.

Thank you to Andrée for wise words and advice, so appreciated.

Finally, I would like to thank all the wonderful people I have met and the friends I have made since I moved to Dublin so many years ago and really are too many to mention. To the ladies in my bookclub who are the most wonderful inspirational friends! A special acknowledgement to the ladies of the Foxfield Sutton Ladies Society who have shown me that age is only a number and life is to be enjoyed. Also, to Carol and the joyful St Brigid's line dancers who show that dance is truly uplifting, no matter what age you are.

Finally thank you to all the frontline workers who have kept going through the crisis of the pandemic. Society owes you all a huge debt of gratitude.

Jane

About the Author

Jane Carson is originally from Kent and moved to Dublin nearly 25 years ago when she married her Irish husband. She is the mother of two grown up children and is the unpaid servant to two thoroughly spoilt dogs.

In addition to writing Jane is a botanic artist. She had long thought of writing, but it was only when she joined the Write of Passage Growth Academy and connected with fellow writers that her dream became a reality. The Cactus Growers' Club is Jane's debut novel.

Printed in Great Britain
by Amazon

71723052R00139